D1287705

BRYHER

GATE TO THE SEA

—

PANTHEON

The photographs of Paestum in this book
are by Islay de Courcy Lyons

TO KENNETH AND ISLAY

"After the death of Alexander at Pandosia in 326 B.C. the city fell again under the complete and undisputed power of the Lucanians. From that moment its unfortunate inhabitants reverted more and more to barbarity: they were even forbidden to speak Greek, and they only gathered together once a year to recall with tears their ancient greatness, and to call each other by their old names."

P. C. Sestieri, *Guide to Paestum*

". . . the Samian priestess at a yearly ceremony secretly made off with the idol of Hera and hid it in a lonely place in the woods by the shore, in the midst of a withy brake, where it was then re-discovered and cakes were set by its side, possibly as bridal offerings."

Quoted from Athenaeus, in L. R. Farnell,
The Cults of the Greek States

Further reference note that the chief festivals of the Goddess were held at Argos, that Hera was the goddess of religious song, that she was attended by sixteen matrons, and as many girls; "the Argives are called her people by Pindar," and the ears of corn are called "the flowers of Hera."

L. R. Farnell, *The Cults of the Greek States*

IT WAS NOT SO DARK AS IT HAD BEEN A MOMENT before. In an hour dawn would rise over the sleeping city. Nobody was abroad. The few people officially awake were the sentinels on the Gates, one facing the mountains, one the sea, while two others, to north and south, overlooked the plain. Most of the Lucanians had left on the previous evening to hold their annual Games in honor of the god of war, and part of the silence was due to Poseidonia's being almost empty. Only the slaves and the aged remained inside the walls.

Lykos tried to turn without waking his wife, who was lying beside him. The pain in his leg was growing worse. They could still breathe in their corner, which had been the doorkeeper's shelter, but presently the sun would beat through the thin roof until it would become impossible to sleep upon the brazier-hot floor. He tried not to think about their former home or the cool myrtles growing up the courtyard wall. Why had he been the best netmaker in Poseidonia, why had he won the boys' foot race at fifteen, to end without a rag that he could call his own, less valued by his masters than a dog? It was like the pavement in the atrium, white in one half, black in the other, all happiness, all misery, as he thought whenever he swept it; and now the day that was about to come was spoilt. It was the solitary festival when the slaves might speak their own language without being beaten, and worship again in temples that had formerly been their pride. He had thirsted for this moment as a traveller for a mountain stream until he had heard his master say brutally to the steward on the previous afternoon, "At least the Games give us a chance to rid ourselves of slaves that are no longer sound." His leg had given way twice during the previous week, and once, to save himself from falling, he had grasped at a vase and broken it. Suppose his owner wagered him upon the luck of some Lucanian's arm, and the swordsman lost? He would be torn from Phila and would never see her again.

He could bear the pain and the losses, Lykos

thought, though his fingers went to the lobe of his branded ear, so long as they were not separated. Hera, the Lady, whose great Temple had miraculously escaped the fire, had blessed their marriage. Other men grumbled about their wives, called them scolds, wasteful or miserly as the case might be, but in spite of her gray hair and thin, worn face, Phila was the same to him as the day when she had waved from the wall (and she had had to climb a tree to get there!) when the citizens had brought him home from the foot race, crowned with wild olive. If it had not been for her, he would have tried to escape. A few men had got across the mountains to Salente, though more had been killed on the way. She had dragged him into shelter after the battle, she had nursed him and hidden him, so that he had not been sold to some foreign slave dealer but had remained at least in his city; yet now, in her old age, he could neither protect nor console her. He had sinned, yes, he had not believed until too late that the Lucanians would attack them, but it was so bitter, so implacable a punishment, and he groaned.

The straw rustled under his stiff leg. He knew that Phila was lying almost on the floor but she had begged a pad of old cloth and slipped it under his knee to ease him. He must be feverish again, the buzzing in his head rumbled into cheers, he was racing along the sand, balanced against the air in a long, continuous movement that lifted him above

11

the ground. Only the weight of his breath had kept him from flying like a bird. There had even been talk of sending him to Corinth. Perhaps he had been proud, but could you ask a boy to be indifferent while the judges placed the olive crown on his head? A spear flung by an unknown Lucanian as he was defending the street in front of the dolphin fountain had stopped his running for ever. He would never know that glory again; oh, he did not mean the "Ly-kos, Ly-kos" of the shouting crowds but the sensation of being almost out of his mortal skin. That, perhaps, although he had felt it in all reverence, had been pride. His lameness was as final as death, and if, as men said, the end was the extinction of being, he would never know ecstasy again, even among the shades. A traveller had once spoken to him of the mysteries; they promised a further life to their initiates, but he was a plain man and all that he had asked of Fortune was to stay with Phila, make his nets, and grow old, in obscurity and contentment. Phila would have answered if she had been able to read his thoughts, because she was lying awake beside him although her eyes were closed, "All you would have asked! The sun, moon, and stars! What you are praying for is eternal happiness."

Phila had hardly slept at all. Her fellow slaves had discussed the possibility of Lykos' being sold for weeks past, in front of her; it was strange how misfortune brought out the evil rather than the good in people. Once when she had been sent to the market for some meat, she had slipped into the Temple and had begged Harmonia, the high priest-ess, to intercede with the Lady, Hera. "I have noth-ing," she had murmured; but Harmonia had an-swered compassionately, "It is the prayer that matters, not the offering." Poor woman, Harmonia had sorrows of her own to bear. Her father had been one of the leading citizens of Poseidonia, and she had grown up in this very house. Some of the servants still remembered her grave beauty as a girl and the surprise in the city when she had dedi-cated herself to lifelong service at the Temple. It was said to have been in expiation for the misfor-tune of her brother. That foolish boy! He had wan-dered accidentally into a sanctuary in the moun-tains, and the Immortals had stricken him with occasional fits of madness. His father had spent a fortune making atonement for him in temple after temple, but the gods had been implacable. Some-times he had rushed exuberantly to join the youths of his age at their games; then for no reason he had darted away, flung himself on the sand, and brooded for hours over a cockle shell with his cloak almost covering his head. Yet he had fought with his com-rades during the battle, and it had been "mad Archias" who had led the survivors to the wharf and sailed with the last ship toward Salente and freedom.

Phila had prayed. Their fate now was in the

13

hands of Hera. There, in the darkness of the almost deserted Temple, she had remembered that once in a similar case some merciful hand had given the couple a draught of hemlock so that the Lucanians, the next morning, had found them beyond the reach of pain or separation. "Pity us," she had begged Harmonia, whom she had found again in the aisle and to whom she had told their story. The priestess had looked at her sadly for a long time before she had answered, "It is dangerous because you are the property of a Lucanian. I must consider the matter. Come to me after the ceremony at the festival." If only the priestess would give her such a phial, they would take the rest of the day, crowding the good things of age into it without its aches and agues; yes, they would sit on the bench in the courtyard and remember the things that Lykos had loved, the foot race and his wreath, the stalk that had caught his black hair into a great curl that was like a horn above his flushed face, everything except their former home. There the roses that she had planted had been torn up, the awning burnt, and the garden where he had dried his nets had been destroyed to make stables. She did not want to disturb her husband, whose head was turned toward the wall, but she could not help her hand touching his arm; it was as light a pressure to Lykos as the olive leaves had been, although he did not move because he supposed her to be still asleep.

14

It was too early to wake Phila yet, Lykos was thinking; he must be patient. Nobody was left who could intercede for them; he would not go to that traitor, Phanion, whom the Lucanians had captured in the hills as a boy and whom they had installed as high priest after the conquest. He was more Lucanian than his masters. If some wretched captive begged him to mediate with his owner, Phanion's favorite reply was that adversity was a better teacher than the philosophers. No, their only hope now was that Harmonia would be merciful. He loved the sun, the splash of water; oh, how he longed to feel the waves before he died. But what would he do without Phila? He was lame, the conquerors were not fishermen and they wanted neither boats nor nets; they had forbidden him to speak his language. If the Lucanians had searched from Asia to the Hesperides they could not have found a finer weapon to destroy the city. The very sounds that were a man's earliest memories had been taken away from him, nor might a mother hum a Greek cradle song to her child. They could neither resist nor communicate with one another. Oh, what riches they had had, and he was not thinking of the bowl with the white lilies (Hera's flower) floating under the wine as if they grew from the floor of the sea itself, nor of the thonged jars of honey that the sailors had brought to them every year; no, what he was remembering was the right to call the common

15

things of life by their true names, bread, oil, rope, fire. Losing this, rather than the branding, made them slaves. He had been as much to blame as all the other citizens. He had wanted to knot his meshes in peace and forget the unrest in the hills. He had said like so many others among his neighbors, "It is just their leaders. The Lucanians are men like ourselves. Besides, how can they get inside the walls?" The whip scars on his back were a witness to his folly, but like the rest, he had bought his knowledge too late. He felt his wife stir, now he must not wait because he had always been the first to give the greeting. "Phila!" he whispered gently, calling her openly by her name for the first time for a year, "wake up, Phila." The familiar voice answered (how thin, how tired it sounded), "Have faith, Lykos, Hera will have mercy on us."

The light woke Harmonia. She started up guiltily, knowing that she had overslept. What an omen on the Day of the Ceremony! She stretched herself, poured water into a bowl to bathe before the ritual prayers, and hoped that Demo, that tiresome girl whom Phanion had insisted must be trained as her first attendant, was not already waiting outside to jeer afterwards about the tardiness of her mistress.

It was still early enough for the cold water to make her flesh shrink as Harmonia dashed it across each shoulder in turn. While she was numbering over the events of the previous day as Nikias, her first teacher, had trained her to do while bathing, she was aware of a more than usually oppressive sadness that came from emptiness and disillusionment rather than from any portent of disaster. The Day of the Offerings! It seemed like any other morning; they were forgotten of the gods. She shivered, she must purify herself after so wicked though involuntary a thought; but tomorrow, not now. First she must accomplish the spring rites at the old shrine by the mouth of the river. Perhaps it was the long fast that had let something so evil cross the unguarded threshold of her consciousness, or was it a deposit from that final, uneasy slumber that had followed several sleepless nights? She yawned, pouring fresh water over her arms, and, in anger at herself, began to dry them harshly with a rough towel when Demo knocked at the door.

Harmonia did not answer for a moment. Such interruptions, even the mere effort now of climbing the Temple steps, distracted her meditation. She could feel closer to Hera if she lived in a hut in the fields, although Nikias had warned her that this was not the wish of the Immortals. "We are the bridge," he had told her during the last, quiet meeting that she had had with him, sitting on a summer day under Poseidonia's famous roses, "and it is the will of the gods that we belong equally to the Temple and the people, never to ourselves." No man had been wiser than Nikias, and the Immortals had rewarded him. He had died in his sleep a few months before the Sack of the city. She sighed, pulled the new-pleated chiton across her still damp breasts, and opened the door, just in time to prevent Demo from knocking again.

"I was at prayer," Harmonia said reproachfully. The girl stared modestly at the ground after her sharp eyes had taken in every detail of the unusually splashed floor, then she answered respectfully, "It is so early that I feared my mistress might not be awake."

Harmonia did not reply. She allowed Demo to help her put on her cloak and adjust the folds, knowing that if the girl had surprised her asleep she would have run to Phanion afterwards with a complaint about ritual carelessness. The fact of the priest's hatred was certain; what puzzled Harmonia was its cause. A priestess had no power. The tiny dole of food during the year, the single dress that they grudgingly allowed her for the ceremony, were not enough to make other women covet her place. Or were they? She was almost the only survivor of the great Poseidonian families who was neither an exile nor a slave. Were the Lucanians still afraid of a name that she had given up, and how long ago, at her Temple dedication? Theron, son of Archias, her ancestor, had given his full strength to the city and perhaps the burden had been too great? Harmonia suspected that generations of stifled rebellions had flared up in her brother, and that it was this, expressed in a form of restless wandering, rather than his innocent entry into a cave during a storm that had chased away his wits. "We must protect the sanctuaries," Nikias had said, "or else some ignorant shepherd will destroy them for the sake of a broken drachma; but the gods never punish a child for any involuntary fault. Your brother has sacrificed, he has been forgiven, it must be another matter that is troubling his mind." Perhaps it was her father's sternness that had produced the fatigue, the sense of separation from the world, that had driven the priestess herself into Hera's service? Demo stood up. Harmonia caught the flash of contempt that crossed the girl's sullen face, and wondered how long it would be until she was summoned from this familiar room to pass the gateway from life to its opposite shadow? Would they poison her, throw her into the sea, or, worse perhaps than either, send her as slave to some hovel in the hills? She walked slowly into the court-yard and over to the niche where, on the previous evening, they had set up the image that she was to carry in today's procession. "Help me!" she murmured, looking at its austere and roughly molded features. The enemy had seized the Temple's gold, the jars of honey, and the sculptured vases but had overlooked the treasure that formerly ten talents could not have bought, a figure of Hera carved from a wild pear tree at Argos and brought by the original settlers. How alone she was! Nikias and her parents, the friends of her childhood, lay under the earth. She had never heard if her brother was still a wanderer or if the sea had flung his unburied bones onto the shingle of some beach. Still all of them were happier than her people here. What answer could she give to that poor woman? It was more merciful to give Phila the hemlock than to let the couple suffer; Lykos had often taken her brother out fishing when Archias had been a boy. Yet to help a slave against his master was a savagely punished crime, and if Phanion heard of it it would give him the excuse that he needed to hand her over to the Lucanians. Their conquerors were a super-stitious people and had been unwilling, at first, to take anything from the Temple but its treasures. Had their feelings changed over the years, and was Phanion afraid that unless he were to prove his usefulness by disclosing some apparent plot, he would be, himself, dismissed?

Harmonia turned away, so that Demo should not see her distress, and as she moved a ray of light fell upon the statue of Hera. She stepped back with a cry. The eyes looked at her, the lips smiled.

"My lady!" She flung herself upon her knees to begin the ritual supplication. The miracle ceased, the aloof head was once again a fragment of ancient wood. It did not matter. At this hour, at the moment when in despair she had doubted her own faith, Hera had remembered her, not with anger, but with compassion.

"Corn ear, flower stalk." Her voice chanted the words but her thoughts were far away, with her mother who had lifted her up, shoulder high, to see the flute players or her little cousins, trotting behind the worshippers with their arms full of blossoms. Then she rose (how her hands were trembling!) and placed the statue reverently in the carrying basket. The first, chief ceremony was to twine it about with rushes at the shrine. The spirit of Hera went from the Temple in spring to roam the meadows like some grave and solitary girl. She would heed no supplications until the women sought her through the fields with flowers and songs to escort her unwillingly home. "You must see it in symbols," Nikias had said; "there is winter, there is spring. The spirit has to renew itself in solitude. There is a moment in every season, every life, when even love is an intruder."

Harmonia lifted the basket. She was shaking with wonder and excitement. During the years of her service as first attendant and then priestess, through the terrors of the Sack and the despair that had followed it, she had isolated herself in contemplation but had never known vision. "It is true that the Immortals speak to us," Nikias had explained, "but

neither often nor always to the people we expect."
It had been the solitary desire that he had been
unable to relinquish, and she knew that it had remained unfulfilled.

Demo opened the door. The city was waking up.
Three girls strolled by, jars on their heads, going
to the fountain. Harmonia was about to step into
the street when she remembered, and paused. "The
token," she said, holding out her hand. Phanion
had promised to send it to her by Demo; otherwise,
as Poseidonians, they were forbidden to pass
through the Gate.

"They know we are coming," the girl said sulk-
ily, "they will not expect it."

"They asked for it last year." She had mislaid it,
Harmonia recalled, and to add to the humiliation
the guard had pointed to it hanging round her neck
while she had been fumbling inside the folds of her
cloak. Demo had to search in her own girdle before
she found the rough bit of metal, and Harmonia
took it with distaste. She hated to touch the greasy,
dirty lump, but she intended to carry it, if only to
prove to Demo that outside Temple matters, she
obeyed Phanion's orders. He had talked for weeks
before the ceremony about the difficulties of getting
permission for them to leave the city, more to im-
press them with his power, Harmonia suspected,
than because of Lucanian objections. The day was
a holiday, and their masters did not care whether

22

the battered, beaten remnant of the Poseidonians had a procession or not. The Commander even welcomed it, the priestess had heard; it kept the masses out of mischief.

Harmonia took a cord from an old robe and strung it through the hole in the middle of the token. She had to wear this round her neck because her hands must be free for the basket and the rushes. What had become of the great silver disk, the emblem of the city that had hung formerly in the council chamber? Some said that Poseidon himself had sent a messenger to fetch it during the attack, and that a spark from his flying sandals had started the fire. Whatever happened, it was lost; the Lucanians had searched for it but it had never fallen into their hands. The thin silver symbols had also disappeared. Some of them had had a dolphin on them, others an ear of corn. Were they hanging up, as amulets, in the hovels along the hills or had they been melted down to provide a man with the cost of his new sword? There was no escape for the vanquished, whether they were objects or slaves. All the Lucanians valued were weapons or horses. It had been useless to repair the wharves because the fleets full of honey, vases, and linen that had come annually to Poseidonia had never returned. They saw no ships, even from the walls, except an occasional local vessel, anchored by order outside in the bay. The crew was never allowed to land;

the Commander of the city did not want his soldiers to exchange news with strangers. He sent instead his heavily guarded rowboats to collect a toll and buy the few things that were needed. How harsh, uneasy, and merciless they were, Harmonia thought, yet the force that the Lucanians worshipped with such devotion had smashed Greek beauty and a search for truth as easily as the wind was scattering the too-open petals of the roses across the pavement in front of her.

The sky was still gray as they walked slowly toward the Gate. Yesterday's dust blew intermittently along the chariot ruts. Demo yawned; it was a full hour before her usual waking time, and the morning had begun with a disappointment. "Go early," Phanion had ordered; "your mistress will be weary after fasting for so many days, and if you can surprise her before she begins the prayers I can tell the Commander truthfully that she is getting too old to carry out her duties." Demo wondered for a moment if she could pretend that was what had happened; with all that water spilled over the floor the woman must have wakened late and sprung from bed hastily, but no, it would be too dangerous. The priestess could swear by the altar of Hera that she had been at her prayers when her attendant had entered. "Take care," Phanion had insisted, "I must have certain proof before I go to Commander Lucullus. I would rather have you wait for a month than arouse her suspicions through some rash or foolish action."

Ah well, another opportunity would occur soon enough, Demo thought, adjusting her wreath that was already a little loose. It suited her, she knew; even the coarse linen of her chiton could not entirely hide the curve of her body, and there was just enough color in her cheeks for a boy to compare them with a flower; she was not tanned to an unfashionable darkness. She knew the priest better than he knew himself. He was a coward; the young men did not like him, and he was afraid of what might happen once the elders died. People said that while he had been a prisoner he had betrayed some weak part of the wall to the Lucanians. Suppose he had, why blame any individual for looking after himself? Phanion was mistaken, however, in thinking that they wanted to stop the ceremony. "Let the slaves have their day, it helps to keep them quiet." You heard this not only from the farmers but all over the city. She looked up at Harmonia—the woman was carrying the statue lovingly as if it were a heavy child—and shrugged her shoulders. How people wasted life! This was the moment to lie asleep on the pillow of some young man's shoulder —Rufus, perhaps, or Patius; only then, alas, a girl had to be Lucanian, and though she was freeborn she came from a village in the hills that had been left at liberty because it had supplied food to the

25

conquerors for years before the Sack. She was not a citizen.

It was so seldom that Harmonia took any but the Temple road that it seemed strangely unreal to be walking down a formerly familiar street. It had changed, the fountain of the nymphs had disappeared, and what was left had the watery quality of common objects remembered in a dream. She had crossed these wide stones so often as a child, holding her nurse's hand on their way to the shore or to play with her companions when she was older. She had followed her mother's funeral here one dark and windy morning, and it was under the niche that she had thought then that Fate had so paralyzed her emotions that she would feel no subsequent doom. Oh, the vanity of it! It had been the solitary consolation during the last years that neither of her parents had lived to endure the Sack. There had been only poor, mad Archias, and among so many who had been wise, strong, and clear of mind he had been one of the few to escape.

Even such memories passed. She was surprised that she felt such indifference to them now, but the present had obliterated the past; it took an effort of will to recall the sorrows and the joys, the hour seemed hollow, the stones another city. Even eight years after the fire it was still full of scars. Most of the trees that had scented the air with myrtle and with jasmine had been destroyed. No courtyard had been replanted; the Lucanians were contemptuous of gardens. A pear tree, perhaps by the will of Hera, survived miraculously beside a ruin. Harmonia looked out for it each year; the sight of the boughs, just visible above a wall, gave her courage. There were so many problems to solve, apart from her personal fate. If she were certain of Phanion's denunciation why should she not be merciful and give Phila the hemlock? For the old, death was more merciful than separation. They still kept a few drugs for the sick, although no pilgrims came any longer, merely a trickle of people from the bordering villages. Yet if it were traced to her, the Lucanians might shut the Temple altogether, and it was the only consolation left to many of the slaves. There was also the question of Philinna. That name had pricked Harmonia's conscience whenever she had thought of it, and that had been often, during her fast.

She had watched Philinna grow from a round child dragging at an elder's hand into a girl so lovely that she might have been one of those nymphs with an apple basket on her head that the shepherd boys sometimes fancied they saw up in the mountains. Her mother was Poseidonian and her father a farmer from one of the border villages that had allied themselves with the Lucanians. Philinna had come recently to beg that she might dedicate her childhood robe and a jar of honey (oh, how Harmonia wished that she had not mentioned this!) at Hera's altar before her marriage. "The neighbors say that the service will not be permitted," Philinna had faltered, "but I was a child when the city fell and Fabricius was a boy, herding sheep in the hills." "Then he is a Lucanian?" Harmonia had asked gravely, and the girl had wept. "What fault was it of ours, the war?" she had protested, twisting the end of her scarlet belt between her fingers. "My mother was Greek, and we desire the blessing that she was given, and my grandmother before her." It had been a difficult decision. Ought she to have said, Harmonia still wondered, "There are other temples for those who have made peace with the enemy"? A few days previously Lykos had passed her door with his face scarred by blows from his master's stick. Yet had she the right to deny the child her offering, not so much a robe as an orderly and happy childhood, because her father had made the best bargain that was possible once the Poseidonians were unable to protect him? He had kept his farm and liberty at the expense, so she had heard, of accepting barbarian customs for himself and his sons. There had been no trace in Philinna's behavior as the girl had knelt in front of her, without a cloak and in the shorter chiton favored by the Lucanians, of Demo's heavy arrogance. That girl looked as if she had never had a man out of her thoughts. Fewer and fewer worshippers came, the poor only or the old, yet the

Temple tradition had to be kept without compromise in these alien surroundings or it would die, and such a dedication could bear no fruit. Once Philinna was part of a purely Lucanian household the husband would see that his children followed his belief. Mercy had held the balance. Harmonia had felt unable to send a worshipper away. She had allowed Philinna to bring her gifts, hoping that she had neither been influenced by the dark gold honey in its earthenware jar nor by the girl's mountain beauty. Only the Immortals could be certain that decisions were impersonal.

She had been thinking so deeply that she was surprised to notice the Gate in front of her. "The sea!" Harmonia could not help murmuring; it was the first time that she had seen it for a year because Poseidonians were allowed neither on the walls nor to leave the city without the permission of their masters. A young guard stepped forward. His helmet made him look taller than he was, and two red plumes swept from their holder over the bowl of the casque in a semicircle above his shoulders. One brown hand swung idly across his short, white kilt; the other held a spear. He advanced courteously because he had been warned of Harmonia's arrival, but had it been some ragged slave trying to slip away during a steward's absence he would have knocked him down with the butt end of his weapon or stabbed him without mercy.

Harmonia slipped the token from her neck and

held it out. The guard looked gravely at the almost indecipherable emblem scratched faintly on one side, and as he examined it she realized that he was Fabricius.

Harmonia would not have recognized him if he had not come up the last few steps to meet the women after Philinna's dedication. Even then, she would not have noticed him had he not run up to Philinna's mother, bent, old, Greek as she was, with the gift of a new headcloth. Now, looking at his rather solemn youthful face and remembering this act of kindness, Harmonia smiled.

"Pass in peace."

"May I keep the token?" Hera must have put the words into her mouth. "We return by the Gate of the Towers because this path is too narrow when there are many worshippers."

Fabricius hesitated. It was usual to deposit such tokens at the guardroom, but it was a reasonable request. The priestess was not leaving the city, she was merely going for an hour to a dangerous and tumble-down old shrine, and she had probably been told to surrender it on re-entering the town. "Remember to give it up," he cautioned as he handed it back. The woman had been kind to his Philinna, he reflected, although now that the girl was his wife he had had to forbid her to attend ceremonies where the rest of the worshippers were servants. Then, because he felt as confused in front of Harmonia's dignity as he had felt when the commander of the army had spoken to him during a night watch, and because he knew that Philinna missed the Temple, he half saluted and muttered a second time, "Pass in peace."

It gave Harmonia an illusion of freedom to be outside the walls. In front of her was the wreckage of a wharf. The Lucanians were not sailors and had left the storms to finish what the battle had begun. The sea was still gray in the early morning light. "Look, Demo, there is a ship anchored in the bay!" she said in a puzzled voice.

"The talk is that the smiths are short of metal." Demo gossiped with everybody. "They are forging spearheads for the new company of the Guard."

"Or could the captain have come here by mistake? It's a trader, not a fishing vessel." They had seen no boats other than the local craft for years.

"Oh, no," Demo answered confidently, "Lucullus arranged for the cargo to be unloaded while his men were at the Games. The sailors might be Greek," she added, looking slyly at her mistress.

Harmonia was careful not to answer. Any comment might be repeated in a twisted form to Phanion. She noticed now that some soldiers were waiting for a heavily laden rowing boat at a place where some half-submerged blocks still gave a little shelter from the surf. She longed to wait until it landed just to see a Greek face again, but she dared

31

not stay; besides, it was foolish to imagine that the rowers were other than men whose State was their ship. No Poseidonian would risk coming thus near even for a last look at his city. She adjusted the weight of the basket in her arms and walked resolutely along the path.

This was the place where the final stand had been made. Men had locked their shields and faced in each direction while a screaming mass of fugitives and eventually the surviving soldiers had rushed to the last ship. Rescue had been a matter of chance. The elderly potter from the Temple workshop had escaped, his son had been left among the wounded. Three men had dragged their injured captain on board; a group of slaves and dancing girls, owing perhaps to their fleetness, had got away, while their barrel-shaped owner had sprawled under a fallen pillar halfway up the road. Small boys had scrambled down ropes, a man had snatched a baby from its mother when the woman had fallen with an arrow through her head, but nobody among the abandoned wounded had known exactly afterwards who had escaped and who had died in the great fire that had leapt from one timbered roof to the other along the narrow streets. "Archias," the potter's son had gasped, as Harmonia was giving him water just before he had died, "I saw him hold the Lucanians back till his comrades were aboard; then he jumped onto the deck and cut the moorings with an ax."

It was quiet enough now. Nobody went near the beach, and the shrine itself was half an hour from the city, a tumble-down building used only on this one day of the year. Even the path was obliterated by drifting sand; it ended suddenly in the middle of a dune that was covered with low, thorny shrubs and infested with vipers. It was actually Demo's duty to go ahead of her mistress, rattling a stick because Harmonia needed both hands for the statue, but the girl was a coward, the priestess reflected with some amusement, and was already a dozen paces behind her. It was also her first experience as attendant on such an occasion, and she wondered what Demo would do when she had to stay by herself during the next stage of the ceremony. Harmonia had to be alone to weave the rushes into their pattern while Demo had to find the women, supposedly wandering through the fields in search of Hera, and bring them to the shrine with songs.

Something rustled; Harmonia stopped, a viper hissed, hook-shaped on a slab of stone not a twig's length from her sandals, before it glided away between some rocks. "I'm going back," Demo screamed; her garland had fallen forward over her forehead and one flower stuck up grotesquely behind her ear. "I'm not moving a step further."

"Then you'll get bitten. The bushes behind us are full of snakes, it's safer at the shrine and nearer the road." Harmonia hurried on, stepping from patch to patch of open ground as carefully as if she were finding a way out of a labyrinth; she could not confess it to her companion, but she was frightened herself. The air seemed full of warnings that her life as priestess was at an end. Her detachment perished, she could not concentrate upon the prayers, a deadly, malignant atmosphere that she could almost touch rose from the thorns and flies. Then suddenly she saw two pillars in the distance and, freeing one hand, helped Demo to scramble up a bank of shingle to higher, open ground.

"You have your stick? Good. Stand here, and as soon as you see the procession, start the hymn." The girl was trembling, and Harmonia added reassuringly, "We are out of danger now and all of us return by the Gate of the Towers. Lead them slowly forward; remember, many of the worshippers are old."

Demo nodded. She watched her mistress walk toward the little building as if the stony and infested land were a green meadow. Phanion was right, the woman was crazy, and if, as they said, mad dogs left such people alone, perhaps for the same reason no serpent would sting her. Oh, how she wished that she were safely back in the city. It had seemed such an easy task when the priest had stopped her near the fountain and had asked her to watch Harmonia for him. "The poor woman neglects her duties, but I must have evidence before I can

ask the Commander, Lucullus, to dismiss her."
Now, Demo thought, after stumbling into holes,
scratching her feet, and being almost poisoned by
that black, vicious head (she rattled her stick and
glanced about her anxiously), it would have been
safer to let Phanion do his spying himself, in spite
of the reward. "Child," he had continued while she
had rested her heavy water jug on the wall, "you
are verily a blossom of Hera. Do what I ask and we
will see if we can arrange a marriage for you."
Husbands were scarce in Poseidonia unless a girl
were Lucanian born.

Harmonia glanced round after walking for some
minutes to see if her attendant had run away. Demo
was standing stiffly, her head turned toward the
town, obviously too frightened to move. The priestess wished that she herself had a hand free for a
stick. The year before, a viper had been coiled
round the altar although there had been none on
the path. How remote it was! She wondered if any
wanderer had come this way since the previous
festival. It was the haunted landscape of a battlefield abandoned by the gods. She trod on a bit of
brittle wood and jumped as it snapped. Then as she
looked down at the broken pieces, she stopped in
horror. A pole's length away the winter gales had
stripped the sand from a shallow grave, and a white
skull stared at her. She even had the illusion, full
of anxieties as she was, that it knew her. Was it a

boy whom she had last seen driving proudly past in his chariot or a fisherman surprised by the invaders as he came peacefully home with his catch? Scarlet rein or homespun net, both were alike to death and the Lucanians; even the sand was too indifferent to hide the body, and she dared not go nearer to cover the bones lest she pollute herself before the ceremonies. Oh, what had Poseidonia done to deserve such sufferings? "We were free-born and are become as beasts," Lykos had said. "We bribed them and talked of peace, thinking our walls would save us. Why couldn't we have armed and saved our liberty in time?"

The shrine itself marked the landing place of the first colonists above what had formerly been a river full of reeds. There had been some story of an oracle, Harmonia had heard it from her grandmother, if the stream dried up or the rushes ever failed, Poseidonia would disappear. Perhaps the solitary clump in a trickle of water was an emblem of the survivors? Phanion had had to get permission to send a Lucanian boy to the hills on the previous day to cut enough for the decking of the statue. She could see the bundle now; it was lying beside one of the pillars.

She had almost reached the edge of the sea, that smooth, shining ocean that no man could stop from flowing to the beaches where children played happily and no head turned uneasily at the sound of Greek. This was the place where captains and traders had met to bargain and talk in front of little taverns with striped curtains and climbing rose trees planted in red earthenware jars. She lingered for a moment to look at the waves; even if her fears were groundless, it would be a year before she saw them again, the walls hid the bay from the center of the town although she could sometimes hear the roar of the surf on a stormy winter night.

It was the one moment of the whole ceremony when Harmonia was by tradition alone. She dared not ask for another vision after so much had been granted her, but she was in desperate danger and it was hard to drop mortality enough to meet it with indifference. The smile of Hera was eternal, although it had lasted no longer than a flash of the dreaded lightning; she would be helped, Harmonia knew, to bear the degradation and dismissal, but she longed for a familiar face or somebody whom she did not have to comfort. She, herself, would be merciful now that the end was so near; Phila should have the hemlock as soon as the service was over. She worked quickly, weaving the rushes around the figure while she murmured the customary prayers. The head itself was left free, to be crowned by the worshippers with garlands. Yet her thoughts flew in wild circles round the future as well as the past; what would Phanion do, what would become of her, why were her hands for all their training so clumsy and so slow?

"Harmonia, do not be frightened, Harmonia...."

37

A man stepped from the side of the altar and stood in front of her. He was wrapped in a peasant's beehive cloak and had a big straw hat on his head. There was no mistaking him although he had left as a youth and there was now a streak of gray through his dark beard. "Archias, oh, my brother!" She flung herself into his arms, and felt the compassion of Hera flowing through her as Archias stroked her head.

"Did they leave you in peace? How you must have suffered."

"It was so long"—she could not help clutching both his wrists—"it was so long. . . ."

"Yes," Archias answered, looking at her gravely, "it was eight years."

The white face of the dying boy who had told her of her brother's safety flashed into her mind; then Harmonia stepped back in terror. "Oh, Archias! Why have you come back? The Lucanians will kill you if they find you."

"I have been to the Oracle."

"The Oracle?"

"Yes, to Cumae. After we landed at Salente I was helpless from wounds, but my mind was clear. The gods be my witness, I never meant to enter that sanctuary and I thought that after all the misery I had seen, I was forgiven. Do you remember Iphion?"

"Our cousin?" They had gone to the quay to

watch Iphion sail some years before the war. People had laughed at him for giving up his house in Poseidonia and moving his goods and family to the north.

"Yes. He took me into his home and treated me as if I were another of his sons. One night I dreamed of a ship with a star above it beckoning me, so as soon as I was stronger he spoke to Krantas—he was the captain who had rescued us—and I sailed with him on his next voyage."

"How strange! Whenever I thought of you, I seemed to see you in the middle of sea birds and waves."

"I think the gods are merciful to a seafarer, though Iphion said it was the hard life that kept my wits from wandering. It was during the winters ashore that I had disturbing dreams, and so last season, as soon as we had anchored, I went to Cumae."

"And they healed you?"

"It was a perilous journey to make in the autumn, but when people saw from the emblem on my cloak that I was travelling as a suppliant, they neither harmed nor robbed me. Later, when we have time, I must tell you about my experience at the sanctuary; it was as terrifying as a battlefield. The auguries were favorable, so they purified me and gave me two tasks. After I have accomplished them, I shall be as free from fear as a child."

"What have they ordered you to do?" Harmonia asked. There had always been some rivalry between Cumae and themselves, but she had heard that they had a priest who was especially gifted in calming troubled minds.

"First, I have to rescue the disk of our city. Some of the exiles want to found a new settlement, but they cannot sail without some legacy from their ancestors. Do you remember the morning of the Sack? I asked you to come with me, but you would not leave the Temple."

Harmonia nodded. Even now she could smell the smoldering boards, the blood, and the water-soaked, half-burnt hangings. "I had my duties," she said, just as she had answered that day, eight years before, when she had last seen her brother.

"I took my place beside our Commander, but he gave me the disk and told me to take it to you for safety at the Temple. I could not get near, the flames were so high that there was no way through them, and I was blocked some steps from our house. I rushed there and buried it in our courtyard with our own jewels. The javelins were whistling over my head and it was not for myself that I hid the treasure but to save it from the Lucanians. I never expected to see another sunrise."

"It's impossible," Harmonia stammered. "How did you ever get here?"

"Did you see the ship in the bay? Krantas is captain of it. He believed me"—Archias did not add that most of the inhabitants of Salente had doubted his story—"and he will wait for us until an hour after sunset. I landed in a small boat about an hour ago. There were just enough rushes left for me to hide it."

"And the second task?"

"I was to tell my sister, the interpreter of the oracles said, 'Loyalty is to Hera, not to a place.' He explained that I was to take you to Salente."

"To Salente!" Harmonia echoed. It was as sudden as the smile had been that morning; yet if she died or if Phanion had her banished to the hills, he would destroy the figure that had come from Hera's own city of Argos or fling it into a hole in some field. He believed the statue to be the rallying point of resistance against the Lucanians, and for once he was right. "But how are you going to get in or out of the city," she continued, "or if there, dig up the disk?"

"Not many fugitives have reached us, but a man told me that he escaped by mingling with people from the villages after the ceremony last year."

"It might be possible," Harmonia said doubtfully. "We only allow women, as you know, but the guards do not care. There are always a few men who join us near the Gate and leave us directly we are inside the town. They would never see their relatives otherwise, although they live within sight of the walls, so we do not object. But suppose somebody recognized you?" she added anxiously. Children had betrayed their parents, and wives their husbands, through sheer terror.

"Not in this cloak!"

It was true. Who would associate the gaunt figure in his peasant clothes with Archias, the young student, who had worn the whitest, thinnest tunics in Poseidonia? Yet had the Oracle really imposed so stern a task upon her brother, or was it a subtler way of telling him that a broken mind could be healed only by death? "It is impossible," she murmured again.

"Who is at our house?"

"The Lucanian Commander. He is away at the Games, but he has a dozen slaves." Perhaps the solution would be for them all to drink hemlock together; then Harmonia gasped, remembering Phila. "There is one chance," she said. "Is your boat big enough to take two more survivors?"

"It depends, it is rather small. Who are they?"

"Do you remember Lykos? He took you fishing when you were a boy." Archias nodded and Harmonia continued, "He is now the Commander's slave, but the steward wants to sell him because he is lame, so his wife asked me to give them hemlock. Perhaps they could help us." She started; she had said "us" and not "you."

"How soon can I speak to them?"

"Not until after the ceremony. I shall see Phila then and will bring her to you."

"I will wait for you outside the Temple."

"No, that is dangerous. Besides, now I live further away." They had evicted the priestesses from their dwelling shortly after the city had been sacked. "Do you remember the fountain of the dolphins?"

"Night after night I walk around Poseidonia in my dreams."

"My room is near and there is a little garden opposite where you can hide. Is the boat really big enough? How did you manage to get it through the surf alone?"

"I wasn't alone. Come here, Myro."

A boy emerged from the corner of the shrine. He rubbed his hand through the short, brown hair that was stuck together by salt and stared at Harmonia, she thought afterwards, as if she had just returned from the shades. There was a patch down the front of his fishing tunic, and he seemed to be about thirteen. "It is Iphion's child," Archias said. "Do you remember him?"

"I knew your father," Harmonia said kindly, amazed that her brother should have brought so young a creature into such peril. "I did not know that he had another son. The one I met was older."

"He . . . it . . . Myro is really a daughter," Archias said as if this surprising fact was the most ordinary event in the world. "Nobody else wanted to come and I had to have some help. I think a boat must have been her cradle, she is never happy out of one."

"My name is Myron, not Myro," the girl said firmly, stressing the masculine form of the name. "I am a boy and I am going to be a sailor and go with Archias on his voyages. Have no fear," she added, turning with such complete assurance toward Harmonia that the priestess smiled, "we shall rescue you by nightfall."

"Archias! Are you still mad? How could you bring the girl here?"

There was a sudden sound of voices and flutes; the procession had reached Demo and begun the opening hymn. "Hurry, you must hide." Harmonia looked wildly round at the bare slope.

"My master is not mad," Myro protested indignantly; "he sees visions, and because other citizens are too stupid to perceive them they think he is ill."

"You must go, Archias, there are no men among the worshippers, you are doubly in danger."

"Have no fear, it is the will of the gods."

"Follow the course of the stream, there is a path near the little village that leads up to the Gate. Go, they are almost here."

"Come." Myro tugged at the man's cloak and pushed him through a hole that Harmonia had not noticed at the side of the shrine where a piece of timber had fallen and had never been replaced. "We shall wait for you by the dolphins," the child assured her in a loud whisper before wriggling head foremost after him through the opening. Harmonia turned and took up her position in front of the statue. How confused she felt, and tired, and now the women were forming in a half circle in front of her. She noticed to her surprise that Aristeia was leading them. Where was Demo? Perhaps the girl had stepped on a snake in panic and been bitten, or had she run away? Suppose they noticed how roughly the rushes were knotted. The last words of the supplication died away, and from habit, because her thoughts were entirely with Archias, she began to chant the prayers.

How familiar it was, yet how changed! Archias stopped to shake a pebble out of his sandal. Could that group of huts be all that was left of the prosperous fishing village directly outside the city? The Lucanians had the instinctive hatred of many hill people for the ocean. Some of the swift Poseidonian ships (they had been the pride of the coast) had slipped their anchors and got away during the surprise attack, but the enemy had burnt the rest. They had only permitted a few fishermen who had acted as their guides to keep some craft that were too battered and old to be sailed far from shore.

It was another reason for hating them, Archias thought. He loved the sea, it had given him peace. His unhappiness had come from the mountains; he looked up at them and shuddered. Why had he wandered up that ravine on that dreadful, ill-fated day? The Poseidonian boys had climbed into the hills when he was young, to prove their courage because it was forbidden. There had always been the danger of meeting some armed Lucanian along the border; there had been wolves and snakes. "Myro!" He looked round, but the child had run ahead; it was new to her and natural that she wanted to see the procession when it arrived. "Myro," he called again querulously in a low voice; he needed her beside him for a moment just to still the uneasiness that was creeping so suddenly and so mysteriously through his mind. Where was he? What was he thinking about? Oh, yes, that day! It had been the eleventh noon of uninterrupted heat. Would he have plodded up that valley that he had never seen before if his comrades had not mocked him for thinking too much and doing too little? The earth itself had been like pitch and the desolate ridges abandoned by beast or bird. It had been too steep to return by the way that he had climbed; he had been looking far and near for some possible track when Poseidon had shaken his trident, and the crust of the earth had shivered. A few moments later the light had perished from the sky, the rains had burst overhead, and dead goats, sticks, broken pots, and uprooted bushes had boiled down the bed of the torrent that he had just crossed as if some monster with a hundred mouths were spitting them into the sea. It was the day that the gods had doomed the city and a victim was needed. He had seen a cave in front of him with no sign of life outside it or within, a flash of lightning had split the tree a few paces from his head, he had sprung as he supposed to shelter and a voice had shouted at him, "Ai! Fool! You have broken the sanctuary of the Goddess!"

"But you found out afterwards that it was the priestess who had spoken to you," Myro always said soothingly whenever he told her the story. "She, too, was afraid of the storm." Perhaps the voice had been mortal, perhaps not; all he knew was that a herdsman had found him on the following morning, daubed with mud and completely out of his wits. His father had offered sacrifices, the priests had purified him, he had gradually remembered who he was. For days he would have no dreams, and then, over his studies or while he was sitting lazily on the beach, the voices would begin to whisper, "Archias, who sent you to the mountains? You are doomed, Archias, and your family with you. What evil thread did you follow to that sacred valley? Better the lightning had struck you than to be neither in the tomb nor out of it. Can you hear us, Archias, can you hear us?"

"Are you an initiate? Have you the right to say

that your sacrifices were useless or that an act of youthful disobedience could influence the fall of a State?" He could still hear the priest's voice ringing in his ears as they had sat in front of the colonnade at Cumae. "Your sickness is pride." He had not dared look up at the stern face but had waited a little sleepily while the smoke from a fire of autumn leaves had risen into the air. "Obey the instructions that I have given you, and the fears will vanish. Fortune awaits you on the seas, but remember"—he had had the impression that the priest was smiling at him—"you are to keep away from all mountains."

"Look, Myro!" At last the child had run back to join him again, "I know that clump of olives." It had survived but it had not grown. He had no fear now. Hera would show them the way, they would sail in triumph to Salente, and how he would laugh at the mockers who had wanted to shut him up and had even pretended that he had never been as far as Cumae at all.

"They are coming!" Myro tugged at her companion's cloak. She had had two wishes as long as she could remember: to see Harmonia, whose courage had made her a legend to the exiles, and to enter Poseidonia itself. She had been born there but she had been a baby in her nurse's arms when her family had left for Salente, and the city had become in her imagination a place of immense beauty waiting to be freed. One desire had been granted: she had never seen a woman as lovely as Harmonia, but they should have rushed her to the boat, there would have been just time, and left the disk for another year. Archias was always troublesome. If he got an idea fixed in his mind, she had learned not to argue with him. It was better to distract his attention and then, after a while, he forgot his obsession.

"There used to be a wagon drawn by a team of white oxen," Archias said.

"With golden harness." Myro had heard the scene described so often by her nurse that she felt as if she had seen it.

"The highest-born children used to come with the first roses, and it was an honor to walk in the procession." The man stared sadly at the ragged girls; they straggled all over the path and their field flowers were already withered. A celebration could be poor in form yet rich in spirit with the life of its own village, but this was a mockery of what had been; for the first time he realized that Poseidonia had really ended, it was less than a broken strap that a hunter threw into a stream or the empty shells that he kicked over the shingle.

They were standing beside the road because there were several small groups waiting in front of the Gate, but there was little fear of recognition, the people obviously came from different farms.

"Harmonia!" Myro shrieked in what was meant to be a whisper as the priestess walked slowly past them. She was very pale and looked, the child thought, as if she were made from an ivory the color of light. What did the rags or the absence of oxen matter? Harmonia was Hera's messenger, and had the walls opened at a sign from her uplifted hand, Myro would have followed her without surprise.

Harmonia glanced around; she had seen the pair but dared not greet them. She knew perfectly well, both from a long experience with his moods and from the distracted people who had streamed to her after the Sack, that Archias had by no means recovered his wits. Yet unless he were mad, would he have returned to Poseidonia to fetch her? And why had he brought the girl? The poor creature was standing there with an enthusiasm that she had not seen for years, apparently unaware of her danger.

"White osiers joining hill to hill."

The voices blurred as they answered the flutes, and Harmonia noticed with a start of astonishment that the younger people had difficulty in pronouncing the words. Greek had become a foreign language, and in a few years nobody would remember it. It was time to leave (she hoped Hera had sent this thought to her); what could she give to this handful of survivors? They died, or as they got older they

50

were sold cheaply among the bordering farms. Yet was it possible that her will to live was still so strong that she was actually thinking about Salente instead of the prayers? It would feel so extraordinary to be free. Would she ever learn to talk again without looking behind her shoulder or pausing to choose each phrase in case some simple error brought an accusation against a friend? She dropped one of the flowers that she was carrying because now that she had seen Archias she felt that she could not bear the loneliness any longer and her thoughts were wandering. But how hopeless it was! How could they possibly leave?

"Help us to bear our sorrows,"

the women wailed appropriately as they came in front of the Towers. "Where is Demo?" Harmonia whispered to the flute player in front of her as the music suddenly stopped. "Over there." The girl pointed to two figures sitting on the ground to their right. "We found her screaming so a woman took her back as far as the walls; but have no fear"— she smiled contemptuously because none of them liked Demo, who had been forced upon them by Phanion—"she will be well enough to join us when the cakes are served. It was temper as much as her fear of snakes."

The four sentinels lowered their spears. Harmonia put her hand to her throat to pull up the token, but before she could draw it out an officer motioned them to go forward. It was still swinging round her neck when the flutes started a final hymn and the women walked slowly through the gateway.

Myro looked eagerly about her. She was in the forbidden city at last. The exiles had talked about the place as if it had been the Hesperides; they had never settled down. They lived in a group to themselves, trying to keep customs that no longer had any sense, and grumbling, "We shall never be Salenteans," until as her father said it drove the actual inhabitants to shout in return, "But you never try to be." Now that she was older, Myro believed that she understood them. To be an exile was to be like herself. Fortune had flung her into the women's apartments when all that she wanted was to fight Lucanians and sail with Krantas; and when she said that she could not go against her nature, either they beat her or were hostile.

Myro had expected to find the people in tatters, but not this: nobody smiled or seemed to look at the flute players. Whoever they met, even the children, flattened themselves against the wall and stared with blank eyes at the four matrons carrying the statue on a wicker tray just behind the priestess. There was something that she could not describe about the atmosphere; it was not living and it was not dead, it was simply that nothing moved.

The women paused. The fountain of the dolphins

stood forlornly in front of them in the middle of the road. Myro recognized it from her father's tales; it had known glory, fire, and death but it aroused no emotion in her. She had been prepared for danger but not for indifference. She looked up at the sea beast's tail; a figure was clinging to it. As they approached a small and dirty urchin winked at them; it was the first sign of life that she had seen in Poseidonia.

"You may go up the steps if you like," Archias said, "but don't go far and don't get lost." Myro wondered if she ought to leave him. He had had no attacks since he had returned from Cumae but had seemed quiet and almost happy as if he had differed from his fellow citizens only because he saw events from the inside and not merely the surface. How magnificent he had been that morning, steering through the wall of surf toward the calm green of the landing place! Then she forgot her doubts and moved forward with the rest. Harmonia had taken the statue in her arms, and as she carried it up the stone blocks the pleats of the chiton fell into the straight line of a charioteer's tunic when he braced himself for the final, dangerous turn.

Myro gasped. It was the most beautiful figure that she had ever seen in her life.

Most of the men had already drifted away to meet their friends. The rest seated themselves upon the low wall in front of the Temple enclosure. Archias found himself a place where he was partly hidden by a column and could slip away up a narrow street. He was less afraid of being recognized than of having to talk to these half-starved, rough slaves. They reminded him of the beggars that swarmed round a ship whenever it anchored in a foreign harbor. Ah, he had had his share of hardships during the past years and yet, the thought crossed his mind as he stared at the unswept pavement, had he not been happier sharing hard bread and stale water with Krantas than he would have been in the life of philosophical speculation chosen for him by his father? He liked the pattern of waves and sky; even when a pirate ship had sighted them, he had been able to admire the beauty of its sails while he had been sharpening his weapons. That time Poseidon had been merciful and sent a for-once welcome storm so that they had lost their pursuer amid a tumult of water in the darkness.

How familiar it was! Archias looked about him as if he had left the city yesterday. Hermonax had died in that gutter, up the road, beyond the second house on the right. Half the town had been in love with the boy! Yet had a single one of the citizens foreseen, as the youths were strolling home together from their studies through the myrtle-scented streets, that all that beauty would end on a paving stone because a shield was lifted a fraction too

slowly to ward off a Lucanian sword? He had had a
royal pyre, to judge from the scorch marks along
the walls and the rough repairs, or had the women
found the boy and given the body what burial they
could while their conquerors slept off their battle
weariness and the wine? Poor Hermonax! He had
had so much to live for, Archias thought, and he,
himself, exiled and smitten by the gods, so little!
War, peace, day, night—were they not all aspects
of the same implacable circle that would never
change until the gods themselves came back from
Olympus and set their turbulent, unhappy children
different lessons?

There was an even thud of feet. Archias shifted
his position warily in case he needed to slip away.
An officer and four soldiers came abreast of his
pillar; it was the Guard marching back to the
Towers; they lingered a moment to watch the row
of women kneeling on the steps. Archias started to
tremble with rage, then he began to repeat the
words to himself that Krantas had shouted as they
had shoved the boat off that morning, "Prudence,
Archias, whatever they say, *do not answer*." The
men were short and dark compared with his fellow
Greeks, but the yellow plumes swung backwards
from the ridge-holders in their helmets with a contemptuous arrogance, and their spearheads had the
polish of a mirror. One man said something, the
others laughed, then the officer gave a sharp order

55

and they marched away in single file between the chariot ruts toward their barracks. He clenched his fists and thought of the disk.

A beelike murmur floated from the Temple, but there was no sign yet of the distribution of cakes that marked the end of the ceremony. Archias wished that Myro had not left him; she was as far away as she could be, on the top step of all. He sighed; there would be no time to take her along the wharves nor to point out the fountains, but he must show her the place where, after his spear had broken and several had lost their shields, Krantas had shouted, "To the sea!" Some of the wounded had rushed back, leaving a terrified group of women between the barbarians and themselves, but he had rallied a few of the men behind a rough barricade of stones, and they had held up the enemy until the fugitives were on board. "Come now," a sailor had cried. Archias had waited till the last because he had felt absolutely no fear, but he would never forget how, as the rope was severed and the ship began to move, the smoke had risen from the houses along the shore and a tongue of fire had leapt toward their sails. "The Gates of the Underworld have opened!" somebody had yelled, and he had been jammed against the bulwark knowing that his sister was in the middle of the flames. If he could have moved he would have sprung overboard to try to join her, but he had been wounded, although he had hardly felt the javelin that had pierced his arm, and he had sunk helplessly to the deck. Months later, a fugitive from Sele had brought word that Harmonia was alive.

The singing ceased. The four youngest attendants came forward with baskets and began to move slowly along the waiting lines.

"It will be over in a moment," a man said, stretching himself; "there are so few, everyone will get a cake."

"It's merely a survival, what's the use of it?" his companion answered, stooping to flick a blade of grass from between his bare toes. "It upsets the women, they think of the old days and grumble."

"We didn't fall, we rolled right over the precipice. Imagine that great Temple full of nobody but beggars; I've seen the days when the harness of the oxen was plated with gold."

"They would have done better to sell it and hire some good mercenaries. The tolls those traders took from us, and then not all of them had weapons."

"Everybody trusted to the walls. Still, it's a question of riches. Even the Lucanians are getting fat and lazy now, eating our corn and drinking our wine."

"Silence!" A priest in white robes stepped out of a corner and stopped in front of the group. "You are not given a holiday to abuse your masters. Go," he raised his staff in a menacing gesture, "go, or I will have you all whipped."

The men sprang up and fled. One old man stumbled and hit his head against an arch. The priest looked at the Temple with a cold, satisfied smile. It must be Phanion, the traitor, the man who had betrayed the city to the Lucanian army. Archias stood up. A shadow—was it Hermonax or one of the unnamed boys who had fallen here on his shield?—flickered in front of his eyes. He forgot his promise to Krantas, he forgot his sister, something happened suddenly to his throat. Even Harmonia heard the shout as she knelt in front of the altar. It was the battle cry that had not been heard since the defenders had sailed on the last boat, and she turned cold as she recognized her brother's voice, "Poseidonia! Poseidonia! POSEIDONIA!" It rang through the square, it resounded among the rubble and the broken fountains as if it were summoning the stones themselves to rise and resist.

There was the soft sound that a mouse might make in its burrow as men and women rushed wildly from all directions into the square.

Phanion started up in terror at the sound of that long-forbidden, half-forgotten yell. Not only would the Lucanians hold him responsible if they heard of it, but it reminded him of a night that he never wanted to think about again, when he had burst from a burning farm into the middle of a ring of soldiers. Had it been pity for his extreme youth, or had they needed a hostage? He had heard a com-

mand; two men had tied his hands behind his back
and had hurried him off through the woods and up
a steep ravine to their camp. One of his captors had
beaten him savagely because he had accidentally
kicked a stone down the hillside in the darkness.
There had been no other survivors. Oh, those
smoky, flea-ridden huts! He turned his head in-
stinctively and looked up at the mountains. Suppose he had shown the enemy the path to a weak
spot in the walls. Why hadn't the Poseidonians
mended the crack properly instead of letting the
brambles grow up around it? A strong and prosperous city could afford to demand loyalty from its
inhabitants, but he had been alone, his life had
been in constant danger. Had anybody offered him
help? He had known that the town was doomed, so
why should he not have saved himself in the only
way open to him? "Seize that man!" he shouted
angrily, "seize him!"

The women looked round, furtively, guiltily, or
triumphantly, according to their feelings. They
pressed together and linked arms; it made the task
of the few searchers much more difficult. "Such
blasphemy," Phanion snarled, wiping his forehead
because he was trembling with fright. But whoever
the objector had been, the shout had come from
outside the sacred boundary and the person had
immediately vanished.

The murmur of the final prayer was just audible

where Phanion stood. No man had the right to enter the Temple until the ceremony was over, but as soon as the clamor had subsided and the crowd had begun to move slowly away from the square, he beckoned to one of the girls who had been distributing the cakes and sent her to ask Harmonia to meet him in the outer court. He was convinced that the outcry was in some way connected with the priestess, and for the tenth time that morning he repeated to himself that the service was archaic, it contained disturbing elements and it must be stopped before the following year.

Harmonia had already learned from the excited chatter of the flower girls that the man, whoever he had been, had escaped. Poor Archias! He had done exactly what she had feared. Only the memory of her vision that morning and her belief in the sanctity of Cumae kept her from going at once to the cupboard where they kept their herbs. She had one last duty to perform: Phila must have the hemlock. Otherwise her old detachment had returned, and in spite of the peril that she was in she was free from fear. She noticed that her robe was creased from carrying the basket and that there were several willow stains across its white folds. She smoothed it with her hands and went forward to meet Phanion. "You wished to speak with me?" she asked.

"See what your stubbornness has brought upon us," he roared, to the dismay of her two attendants

who had slipped behind a pillar to observe the meeting. "If the Commander hears of this, he will shut the Temple."

"There are no rites of war connected with the Lady, Hera, nor did the battle cry come from a woman's throat."

"You encourage the slaves to remember."

"I carry out the ritual as it has been carried out for generations."

"You give them salves and talk to them about liberty. Liberty!" (The voice was as crazy as her brother's, but much harsher.) "They are better off now than in the days when they were Greeks. Have you forgotten how much hunger there was, and how fewer and fewer ships came to the harbor during the years before the conquest? Now they are fed and clothed and all they have to do is obey. Obey!" Phanion yelled the word as if it were an answer to the shout that had so frightened him. "Why was the city burnt? Because strangers had corrupted it. Who were on the exercise grounds? Not the citizens. They huddled around their braziers spinning words. If a man wore a woollen cloak they called him a barbarian; a lamb, some speculation about the movement of the winds, meant more to them than mending their defenses. And how were the shep- herds to eat if they could not sell their fleeces or the sandalmakers their shoes?"

"I am not a Pythagorean," Harmonia said coldly.

She knew something about the doctrine because Archias had once followed it for a few months, and she had had to nurse him through a sharp fever after he had gone out on a winter day in his thin linen coat.

"Only because you cannot understand the numbers," Phanion sneered. "But Nikias was one, that fool you loved so much. To him a citizen was worth more than his city."

"Why blame me because some wretch, crazy with misery and despair, shouts a cry, that he learned as a boy, in the middle of a group of women?"

"It was Nikias who was to blame, and you are his pupil!" Phanion's face was so distorted with rage that involuntarily Harmonia stepped backward, expecting him to strike her. What could her gentle white-haired teacher have done to provoke such fury?

"It is the name of the city that matters," Phanion screamed. "What has pity to do with it? It is the Lucanians now who are citizens. The Greek survivors will die." He spoke of his fellow countrymen, Harmonia noticed, as if they were a crew of shipwrecked strangers. "Who will remember the fire in another generation? What you call your slavery is an episode."

"I am carrying out the ritual of this Temple. You are not our priest."

"But I am the mediator between yourselves and

your conquerors. Lucullus listens to me. Suppose I tell him that you are too old to carry out your duties." He blurted out in his impatience the secret that he had meant to keep until he had seen Demo. "Perhaps they will let you remain as a sweeper," he added vengefully. "It will be a lesson in humility for one so concerned with prayer. Or . . ." He had to break the spirit of this woman who so resembled the hated Nikias. "There has been unrest lately among the slaves. You know the penalty for encouraging rebellion. It is death."

It seemed to Harmonia that she had been aware so long of what might be about to happen to her that Phanion's threat was like an evocation said with the lips but not from the heart. There had been a smile, Archias had come; even if they never reached it, the thought of Salente was in her mind. "Bring what accusation you will against me. I have never broken the laws." She could still say this truthfully, the priestess reflected. She had not yet seen Phila nor given her the hemlock.

"They will not believe you." Phanion's rage increased; he knew that he had spoken too soon. "If you want to save yourself, tell me the name of the man who shouted that cry."

"It happened outside the Temple."

"And plenty of your women live in the town. Tell me who the creature was before the Lucanians return tonight and I will protect you. I might even

63

persuade them," he tried to speak softly, "to allow your attendants a little more food."

Harmonia bowed slightly. Some instinct warned her to be silent, to gain time. "You suppose me to wield a power that I do not possess," she said after a moment.

"When death faces us, not in a dream but on the battlefield, we do strange things." Phanion continued in so altered a tone that Harmonia looked up in bewilderment; it was almost as if he were pleading for sympathy. "My father took his spear with him from plowing time to harvest, but did your Nikias tell the young men to arm and go and help him? No, he urged the elders to bargain with the Lucanians and abandon the border farms. The men who came from Argos were warriors." He took a step forward as if he, too, were thinking of the wooden statue, almost like the figurehead of a ship, that was standing beyond him in the darkness beneath its knotted rushes. "My father still had the Argos blood in him, and he died."

So it was revenge rather than gain that had forced the man into such treachery? It helped the priestess to understand but not to forgive the suffering that he had caused. "We all lost someone," she murmured, wondering if it were true that the young Lucanians were as anxious to dismiss Phanion as he was to get rid of her. They faced each other silently and then Phanion shouted, as if he

were ashamed of the words that he had uttered,
"See that you send me the name before evening.
Lucullus is angry at the unrest in the town and will
show you no mercy if he thinks you are behind it."

Harmonia walked back toward the small recess
where they kept the bowls for the offerings. She had
noticed the two attendants standing behind the pillars, and she smiled at them reassuringly; they must
have heard Phanion's threats. She, herself, was almost grateful to the priest; his anger had shattered
the half-conscious state that she had been in ever
since she had seen Archias, a feeling of unreality
that had followed her along the road, almost of
having died. Now she was awake, she had only a
brief time to save her mad brother and the statue
that faced her with such tranquillity from its place
by the altar. It had seen the Temple built and the
Cretan ships, themselves now legendary, sail into
the bay, and was so old that nobody any longer
remembered either the hill where the pear tree had
grown or the name of the carver. Any of a dozen
temples to the north, also dedicated to Hera, would
receive it with veneration.

"Do not fear," she said to the women, "I will
pray." They looked at each other, and Harmonia
realized suddenly that in the face of disaster and
crisis she had said the words too often. The Oracle
was right: things came to an end, no matter how

much they boasted that they would keep the spirit alive. If anything were to be saved of a former serenity and richness, growth might begin again at Salente; it was impossible here.

"Did you hear the uproar in the square, Aristeia?" The priestess was longing to know if they had recognized her brother's voice. "I was, myself, in the middle of the supplication."

"I heard the shout," Aristeia answered unwillingly, glancing down at the field flowers that were staining her robe. "It was a man. He must have been at the other side of the road. What have we ever had to do here with weapons?"

"Phanion is convinced that we are encouraging unrest," Harmonia answered wearily. "He is mistaken; if an army of exiles landed from Salente I doubt if a dozen would join them. The slaves are overworked and have nothing to lose, they are muttering not about liberty but bread."

"But suppose he denounces you," Aristeia's companion interrupted, and Harmonia noticed again as she had during the procession that the matron was bursting out of her too-tight dress. "He has great influence with the Lucanians."

"I believe the Commander is less inclined to take Phanion's word than he thinks. I shall ask myself tomorrow to see Lucullus."

"If you are dismissed, all of us will follow you," Aristeia said bravely, because any change at the

Temple would affect her own rank. "The priest would like to stop the ceremonies altogether."

"Another three years," Harmonia said bitterly, "and they will cease of themselves. The children this morning could not pronounce the words of the hymn."

"They cannot practice except secretly, and then the mothers are afraid."

"Possibly the time has come to end them." The women looked at her in such amazement that Harmonia added hastily, "Do not listen to me, I am tired. Perhaps Phanion is right and I am getting too old for my duties. Will you lead the evening procession for me, Aristeia? After fasting two days and struggling through that wilderness this morning, I must rest."

Aristeia bowed her head with a smile of secret pleasure; she was ambitious in a simple way but, unlike Demo, devoted to her mistress. "It is the fasting, my lady. The walk through that dune would have exhausted a young girl."

"At least keep Demo from me, she was troublesome this morning."

"She met us screaming because she had seen a viper."

"She was well enough to eat cakes. I caught her taking a second one from the basket. She thought I had not seen her."

"Phanion sent her here to spy on me. A girl like

67

Demo ought never to be allowed inside the Temple."

"I will see that she does not disturb you," Aristeia said grimly. "I do not even need to shut her in her room. I have only to send her into the courtyard and she will spend her time leaning over the parapet and gossiping with the slaves below, especially today when they are not at work."

The Temple was empty and, now that the flute players had left, ominously silent. The flowers lying in front of the altar scented the air; it smelled green, Harmonia imagined, as she stooped to pick up a rosebud that had fallen onto the pavement. The worshippers had gone to their meal; the harshest of masters allowed them an extra portion of food on this one day, perhaps through some superstitious desire to placate the spirits of the land before the harvest. Her attendants stood aside for her to pass, but Harmonia shook her head. "Do not wait for me, I shall first pray for us all and then distribute the salves to the women waiting outside. Leave my portion in my room and I will eat it later."

The two women walked down the aisle, slowly at first but almost breaking into a run as they neared the court. Harmonia smiled; they were anxious both to receive their share of the feast and to tell their story, with exaggerations no doubt, to the other six matrons. There ought to have been sixteen but the number had been gradually reduced to eight. "May Hera protect us," she could hear them spluttering, "but he shouted at her as if she were a thief and she hardly answered a word."

Directly Harmonia knew that she was alone, she walked back to the statue. How could she break the discipline of years? Now that she had to take off the garlands that were supposed not to be touched until the following day, habit and training were stronger than her sense of danger. She stared at the face; it was covered with a veil. Hoping that the wonder of the morning would repeat itself, she shut her eyes and prayed, but it was a mere babbling of words. If only Nikias were alive to help her! Would he say with a shake of the head, "You are bound to the Temple as long as you can serve it," or—she remembered how his mind had darted from one problem to another, never finding the same solution twice—would he utter just as firmly, "Obey the Oracle. Go to Salente"? She raised her hands to take the figure from its base; they fell again. Her brother would not lie, but might he not have misunderstood or have been drawn back to die here by the homing instinct that brings a wanderer at the end to the place of his birth? Whatever happened, she could not resist the longing to see him once again. She stepped forward, almost unconsciously, and fumbled with the rushes, feeling that a thousand eyes were watching her from the pillars.

"Can I help you?" a voice asked, and Harmonia screamed.

A child came confidently out of the shadow and

patted her arm. It was Myro. "Don't be afraid. Archias is safe. I left him hidden behind the dolphins as you said, but I must go back to him soon. He is restless and troubled."

"I thought it was the girl Phanion sends to spy on me," Harmonia explained, ashamed of her cry. "But how did you get to this place? It is sacred to the priestesses." In spite of the circumstances, she was shocked to see this ragged stranger standing unconcernedly beside the altar.

"Archias told me to find you. I waited outside till your attendants came down the steps, then I dodged from column to column until I was sure that you were alone. You must hurry, Archias may ramble off, he is anxious about his disk."

"I have to take this statue with me."

"You need a knife." Myro looked at the rushes with a professional eye. "Fortunately, I have one."

"We are not allowed to cut anything in this shrine."

To Harmonia's horror, Myro took no notice but slit the swathes from top to bottom. "I do not want to be impious," the child said solemnly, "but it is not safe to leave your brother alone."

"Be careful of the garlands, I have to replace them on another figure. No, child, leave me to do the work, you are not one of my flower bearers. Do you go to the Temple at Salente?"

"I worship Artemis," Myro answered proudly.

There was a little shrine on a headland where the cracks on the gray rocks were filled with rosemary bushes that smelled much sweeter than this heavy incense. She wondered with a sudden stab of unexpected fear if she would ever see it again.

Harmonia untwisted the last thong, looked at the child's determined face, and nodded. "I can see that you would rather worship in the woods than join us in our ceremonies. My teacher, Nikias, used to say that I must remember the differences; what suited the dolphin would only drown an eagle, and so it was with people and their prayers."

"I belong to the sea. I want to be a sailor."

"And what does your father say to that?" It was a strange conversation to have when they were both in utmost danger, and she was disengaging the statue from its wrappings to place it reverently again on her cloak.

"He says it is impossible. But, my lady, now that I have been in Poseidonia surely they will listen to me? I shall die if they shut me up in the women's quarters again. Archias couldn't get anyone else to go with him." She added proudly, "I heard him asking boy after boy."

"Are you not frightened?" There were some small earthenware statues standing against the wall, thank offerings from former pilgrims and of no value to their conquerors. Harmonia picked out the heaviest one, wedged it into the empty space by

71

means of a folded piece of cloth, and began to wind the rushes round its body. This time she made no protest when Myro helped her to fasten the shorter stems.

"Perhaps I was, a little, when the boat almost turned over in the surf, but Archias steers superbly. Even then I thought it was better to drown than to spin."

"If we get to Salente and my words have any influence, I will intercede for you," Harmonia promised, although it was hard to know what could be done with the child. Perhaps her brother could adopt her and take her with him to the Oracle? Myro seemed to have a curious power over the agitated man. Still, there was no time to think about the problem now; she flung the veil over the votive figure and set it up on the platform. Unless somebody lifted it (this should not happen before the following morning) there was little to arouse suspicion. Many of the flowers were already drooping, so that a few extra petals on the floor hardly mattered.

"Influence!" Myro answered in surprise. "But you are a legend in Salente! You could have got away on the ship, and you stayed."

It seemed foolish now, Harmonia reflected, but then she had loved the Temple so intensely that it had never occurred to her for a moment that she would be able to leave it. She had not known enough to realize that the horror would be neither the Sack nor the fire, but the weeks that followed them. A mother's grief for the son killed on the battlefield was simple compared with the anguish of parents and children thrust onto a slave dealer's table to be sold, none knowing the other's destination. And that poor, gray-haired man! A soldier had stabbed him in front of her because, being deaf, he had not obeyed an order. Had her own deep feeling for the city been less service than pride? She swept together the tiny yellow flowers that were the essence of the long Poseidonian fields, and piled them around the altar. "We must go to Archias," Myro pleaded. "If he wanders away he may get lost."

"Could you carry this statue to our meeting place?" Harmonia asked doubtfully. A stranger was forbidden to touch the sacred objects, but the child had already cut the rushes, and once a rule was broken, how easily the next step followed! Her own hands must be free to distribute the ointments; besides, the figure must be taken out secretly. "Be careful"—she put it into Myro's arms—"don't let it touch the ground if you can help." She looked around; there was an old cloak that she sometimes wore hanging in the recess where the medicines were kept. "Fling this over your shoulders, so," she added, "it is too long for you but I have doubled it. Hold the edge firmly in your right hand and if people notice a bulge they will think that you are trying to keep some food warm in a basket. Tell my brother that I have gone to get Phila; she is waiting with the women in the square, but I promise I will join you both directly I have found her."

There was a door at the side that the flute players used. Harmonia opened it and watched Myro run down the steps and into the sunshine. It was noon by now and the streets were empty. The priestess had one more duty. She lifted the lid from an earthenware jar that appeared to be full of camomile. She thrust her hand through the dried blossoms till she felt a piece of linen; under this, tied up in a strip from an old veil, the hemlock was lying just where she had hidden it. It was old; even if she prepared it, she wondered if it had retained its power, but it gave her a sense of security to slip it inside her dress. She had refused it to a dozen suppliants, saying that there was none in the Temple, because she had felt that they must live out the fate allotted to them; but her turn had come, and as she looked at the altar that she would never see again she understood Phila.

It was growing late, yet Harmonia paused for a final moment in the cool, scented darkness. Here she had dedicated, not Philinna's robe (it hung before her now, the blue of a dissolving wave) but her own youth, her longing to seek and see, those great passions that were twins of one another. She was moving now toward exile or death, and as she stared at the indifferent pillars towering above her head, her brother's rebelliousness entered her. She touched a column. How hard it was and cold. Yes, what were they but an episode among the generations? A name might survive; their love, loneliness, and courage were less than a summer shower. "Take Mnemosyne from me," she prayed. "I do not want to remember." Voices echoed in mockery from high in the roof although she knew that nobody was there. "And lose the golden temples," it was almost a song, "forget the Muses?" The familiar aisle was hostile (was this because Hera had already stepped across the threshold and left the dwelling empty for the barbarians?), the priestess shivered, she began to run in panic toward the steps. The whispers followed her: "Was it worth it, the sacrifice? Here I am, lying under a broken beam, and of my four children who is left to bury me?" She heard the moan of a girl: "The javelin was sharp beneath the olive trees." Phantoms joined themselves to sounds until she began to scream as madly as her brother. She dashed into the sunshine, breathed the clear air, and stopped; then as she looked down at the broken city, lying below her in the heat, she remembered Nikias and breathed a final supplication. "What had we done? Tell us the reason for such misery." A lizard scurried across the stones; she saw faces staring up at her and recognized Phila's shawl; then a phrase seemed to echo distantly in her ears, "The road to the mysteries is not a question and its answer. It is as troubled, as unpredictable as the sea."

The light was dazzling after the obscurity of the Temple. Harmonia walked slowly down the steps, unaware that the rippling pleats of her dress and the stiff fold of the cloak over her arm gave the onlookers an impression that some statue had stepped from a pediment to mingle with them for an hour. Half a dozen women, among them Phila, were waiting to speak to her. She could hear them arguing among themselves as she approached.

"It was no mortal voice."

"It was a Lucanian. They wanted to see what we would do."

"It was a drunk slave."

"Where could he get the wine?"

"We were lucky that they did not call out the Guard."

Harmonia looked at the faces; some wanted comfort, others were there out of curiosity. "If you are sick and I can help you, tell me what you need," she said firmly, pausing on the last step, "otherwise the sooner you go to your homes the better."

A few moved away; she gave an ointment to an old woman with cake crumbs sticking to her chin, and reassured a frightened girl. Phila had deliberately chosen a place at the end of the line. "If you want the salve for your toothache," Harmonia said in a louder voice than usual, "you must come with me to my room. We have no more left at the Temple."

"At least the barbarians could have left my lady undisturbed," Phila said indignantly as they started down the road. After the Lucanians had taken over the storerooms and the houses, they had allotted the Temple servants a place in a neighboring quarter of the city. "It does not matter," Harmonia said wearily, knowing that she could never make Phila understand that she had preferred the change. The tiny room was simple and quiet after the heavy scents of honey and flowers (not that there was much of either of these nowadays!), and it was easier to meditate there than at an altar where ritual and gesture mattered more than adoration. Besides, she liked the walk to and fro at dawn and dusk when the columns rose above the desolate town, gray as the sea, yellow as the corn, according to the light. "My lady, you will give me the drug?" Phila panted.

"How do you know what it will be like in the shades?" Harmonia murmured. She was thinking about the conflict between Nikias and Phanion. Much as she had loved her teacher, she had suffered too much during the past years not to know that Phanion had some right on his side although this did not excuse his cruelty. Nikias had seen the best in people. "The Lucanians are men like ourselves," he had said, but this was not true, they were bred to force as the Greeks to speculation, and to them understanding was weakness. What was truth at the end? How much of what she knew in a fragmentary form, from a word, an intuition rising as lightly as a ball and as easily lost, dared she repeat to the anxious figure walking beside her? "Some philosophers say that life is like the palaestra," she suggested; "if we learn what the wrestling offers to us, there will be a crown the other side. Of sleep, not olives."

"Such a thought is for my lady. I cannot understand it. Lykos and I are old. We would rather die together than be separated."

"You are willing to do this for your husband?" Harmonia asked. The dolphin's head facing them upon the side of an otherwise battered fountain was surprisingly undamaged, and she caught a glimpse of Myro's head peering from behind a wall. "It is also dangerous for me. Should Lucullus discover that I have helped two slaves to disobey their master's orders, I and those around me will be punished."

"May the Lady, Hera, be merciful to us all."

"Suppose the steward should change his mind? The sun is warm, and they cannot take the Temple from us."

"They can. Lykos will be sold, perhaps tomorrow; there is no other way than the hemlock."

"There is, but it is a dangerous one."

Her companion looked up in surprise, and as she did so the priestess caught a glimpse of the great beauty that Phila must have formerly possessed before sorrow and suffering had so marred her. "I am unhappy, too, Phila. Phanion wishes to dismiss me from my duties."

"We would never let it happen." The voice was sincere but not startled. She was aware of the rumor, Harmonia thought, everybody seemed to know more about the priest's hostility toward her than she did herself. Yet how could the women prevent her from being dismissed any more than she herself could stop Phila's husband from being sold? She had become too detached, she reflected guiltily, remembering what Nikias had taught, and so, to chasten her, the message had come not in the solemn silence of her own Temple but through a madman and an equally strange child. A stick tapped on the stones, and glancing round, she saw that Lykos was following them. "Yes, Phila," she continued, "I doubted everything that I had learned, and, at that moment, I heard a voice this morning. It was my brother."

"Your brother!" Phila stared as if Harmonia had complained of sunstroke.

"You doubt me? There he is, sitting on that wall."

Archias sprang up; he had been watching them come up the street. The tension had broken with the battle cry, and he was in a gay and reckless mood. He flung his arms round the old woman and kissed her.

"Where is Lykos?" he asked.

"It's not . . . it can't be . . . but it is Archias." Lykos forgot his lameness and ran forward; then he stepped back anxiously, remembering the shout. "Oh, why have you come back?"

"To find the disk."

"That is why, Phila, I said there was another way," Harmonia explained. "My brother has come from Cumae. The emblem of the city is buried under the courtyard of our former house, and the Oracle has ordered him to find it. Krantas, I think he is a friend of yours, is waiting on a ship in the bay. Help us, and we will take you to Salente."

"We shall be put to the torture," Phila groaned, "and I am too old. Oh, give us the hemlock!"

"Torture!" Lykos laughed. "It is going to be difficult but not impossible. Exactly where is the treasure buried?"

"Two paces to the right of the lion, facing the east wall."

"I have sometimes thought that a stone rocked as I trod on it."

"The other slaves will betray us," Phila screamed, clutching Harmonia's skirt.

"Believe in the mercy of Hera," the priestess said, taking the woman's trembling hand. "My brother was sent here by the Oracle."

"We have a chance," Lykos said thoughtfully, "but not much time. The men are going to an assembly at the market place. I left them a moment ago, saying that I did not want to walk so far on account of my leg. The old woman who helps Phila will be asleep, and the dogs know us. I think we can find the disk, but how then are we going to get out of the city?"

"With the people who have come in from the countryside. They are allowed to leave after the afternoon procession."

"If you are missed at the Temple," Lykos asked anxiously, "surely they will send attendants out to look for you?"

"I have told Aristeia that I am exhausted after the fast and that she must officiate. We ought to go singly, however, in case I am recognized."

"Nobody knew me," Archias boasted, forgetting his long absence. "Get Phila to bring you the oldest cloak she has, and pull it well forward over your forehead."

"We can think about such things afterwards." Lykos picked up the stick that he had dropped in his excitement. "If you will wait for us in your room," he said, turning to Harmonia, "we will go to the Commander's house. . . ."

"And join you," Archias interrupted, "with one of my tasks accomplished, in an hour."

The street was deserted. Even the ruins were less splendid than Myro had imagined. Many of the tiled roofs had been replaced by rough boards; there were gaps among the houses, dents in the walls. It had once been swept and clean, with striped awnings and many fountains, but it was not paved with marble and lined with fruit trees as she had imagined it from the talk of the Poseidonian exiles nor was it the citadel (oh, how often Archias had compared it with Troy!) of her father's tales. She forgot that it had no memories for her and that fact and legend were not necessarily twins.

"Wait here," Lykos said. "Watch the road, and if anyone comes, shout my wife's name." He pointed to a place on the wall where Myro could sit. "Phila, perhaps you will stay inside the door; and now, Archias, are you ready?"

The Greek did not move. His eyes were closed, his lips moved, and he was praying silently with a wild expression upon his bearded face. Lykos was not irreverent, but surely this was no time for supplication? "Speak to him," Phila whispered, but her husband shook his head. The man might burst into the battle cry again if they interrupted him suddenly. They stood there, Lykos leaning on his stick, Phila staring up the road in terror because men were approaching, although they were still some distance away, when just in time Archias opened his eyes. "All is well. They have spoken to me," he said, tapping his ears. "The jar is, as I said, two paces from the lion's head at the right of the fountain."

The watchdog growled. Lykos patted it, and it wagged its tail familiarly. "You will find many changes," Lykos muttered grimly, but Archias walked straight into one of the side rooms without hesitation. It had not even a bench in it, only some straw. "Lucullus keeps his hunting dogs where your father kept his rolls and accounts; but hurry, we have less than an hour and it is going to be difficult to loosen these stones."

If Hera willed, the search might be successful, Lykos thought, limping through the rooms. The steward had accompanied Lucullus to the Games; he knew that the slaves were too frightened of him to steal even a drop of oil. The only other woman was older than Phila and asleep in her hovel beyond the kitchen, enjoying that rarest of luxuries, a noonday slumber undisturbed by blows or calls. If Agathias or one of the other servants should come back unexpectedly, he could say that Archias was a gardener, come to look at the old rose tree that now never flowered. "It's a true Poseidonian," Lucullus had sneered, "all promise and no fulfillment." Lykos had left it deliberately untended, not wishing it to bear its blossoms for barbarians to enjoy. He touched Archias on the shoulder and beckoned.

The courtyard had once been full of sweet-smelling bushes planted in earthenware jars. Now it was like a storeroom, with firewood piled in one corner, harness in another; there was only a trickle of water coming through the mouths of the fountain lions, and a dirty strip of what had once been awning lay among a tangle of straps. Archias went straight to the basin, stretched his arms out till his fingers touched the lions on either side of him as he faced the wall, then stepped two paces forward. "Here!" he said, tapping the ground with his sandal; it was in the middle of a block.

"But it's too near," Lykos protested; "those joins have never been disturbed. This is the one that I suspect was lifted." He pointed to a stone in the next row that had sunk perceptibly below the surface. He had swept the courtyard too often not to know every one of its crevices and stains.

"I buried the jar two paces to the right. I remember feeling that the lions were watching me."

Lykos shrugged his shoulders and went off to fetch a pick and a spade. He would have to let Archias have his way at first in spite of the lack of time, but it was natural for a man to forget the exact spot, especially where a battle had been raging outside the house at the time. He came back with the tools and found Archias staring fixedly at the pavement. "It's fortunate my arms are as strong as ever," Lykos said gaily, trying to get the point of the pick into a cleft. "Even the earth here is as hard as rock."

Trembling with terror, Phila walked to the doorway. She had no confidence in Archias' finding the disk; she questioned whether he had even buried it. The poor man! He had angered the gods and was obviously mad. They would be tortured, she could already feel rough fingers on her neck, and though Harmonia had whispered as they left her that she would steep the hemlock, was there enough time left to prepare the draught? How she had longed for the evening! Lykos would have sat beside her on the Temple steps; the saffron of the sky and the green of the pomegranate leaves would have reminded them of the summers when the fleet had anchored at the wharf, and she had protested in vain to Lykos that the scarlet belt he had bought from a sailor was much too bright for a matron like herself. They would have dreamed and drunk to each other, taking a sip of honey afterwards to blunt the bitterness of the draught as their memories sweetened the knowledge of death, and then they would have perished in each other's arms, citizens of Poseidonia, the loveliest city in the world, and however poor the pyre, their ashes would have been scattered in their native place. But now? Even

85

if they reached the north in the Greek boat, what would the future hold for them? They were too old for change. She sighed and stared at the wall in front of her. "How are they getting on?" a clear voice asked.

Phila looked at Myro wearily. "They are digging up the courtyard, but they will never find the jar. What will happen to us when the slaves come back from the market place?"

Myro shrugged her shoulders. She was anxious, herself; they ought to have rushed Harmonia away that morning.

"Do you suppose that he ever buried it?"

"He has always told the same story," Myro answered thoughtfully, "but it must be hard, moving the stones. Suppose I go and talk to him. Sometimes he listens to me."

"Leave him alone," Phila said impatiently; she disliked the urchin, and it was pure impudence to suppose that he could influence his master. "Your duty is to watch the road." She lingered a moment, and then, although she was so tired that she knew she ought to sit down and rest her legs, she wandered back to watch the men digging.

Myro sat, clasping her knees, with her eyes fixed on the house. She was near enough to hear the murmur of voices and the occasional clatter when somebody dropped a spade. Like Phila, she doubted if they would find the jar, although she thought that

Archias had probably buried it. She had learned to distinguish between his stories of the battle—others had confirmed these as true—and the sudden visions that woke him from his sleep and sent him wandering from oracle to oracle up and down the coast.

It was the first time that Myro had really been afraid. She had been anxious when she had slipped away to join Archias on the wharf lest she had not muttered carelessly enough that she was going with a neighbor's cook to market. There had been the possibility that Archias would forget to bring her the boy's clothes, and after he had handed her the bundle she had had to crouch between two great water casks, wondering if they would roll on her, until they were well out to sea. Both of them had been breathless in the boat that morning; she had guessed from her companion's face that he had expected them to drown when a wall of surf had flung their craft almost sideways into a wave. Yet these were surface fears, real enough but bearable. What she felt now was the terror of seeing innocent people, the poor, lame Greek and his sad, suspicious wife, beaten or killed in front of her. If only the exiles could see Poseidonia now, they would want to blot it from memory. No street was safe. The first Greek to notice that Archias had a spade would betray him to the next Lucanian, or if they lingered for a moment in front of the smashed remains of some friend's home a woman drawing water from the fountain would rush to the Guard and tell them that the city was full of strangers. Her family had been right to settle in Salente. "It is what a man thinks and not where he lives," her father had repeated constantly during the early, difficult years before the conquest when those of the family still in Poseidonia had laughed at them. Now she understood how difficult it must have been for him to make the decision. He did not dream, as far as she knew, like Archias. "It was the shrinking of the borders," he had said once; "after the farmers made peace with the Lucanians because we would not help them, I knew the moment had come for me to leave." He had never given any other explanation, and after the exiles had poured in, blaming everybody for their fate but themselves, he had assisted them but had refused to join in their discussions, and had gone whenever it was possible to his property in the hills. She had often heard people speak of him as "Iphion the silent." Yet with such a gift of foresight why could he not see that she had been born to live on a ship and not be tied up like some mischievous puppy in the women's apartments?

In a few moments, Myro decided, she would disobey Phila and go into the house. She must persuade Archias to abandon his search in time for them to get away. Was his plan of mingling with the villagers a wise one? Every Poseidonian knew Harmonia by sight. A charioteer was afraid, not for himself but for his horses, and she saw with a matter-of-fact but still-childish clarity that the mad recklessness that had got them inside the city was about to add to their danger. If Archias could shout the battle cry in the middle of the prayers, there was nothing to prevent him from striding into the market place as they were leaving, and yelling to the un-armed slaves to rise with him against their con-querors. She looked at the small and wonderfully molded lion's head facing her on an opposite pillar, and sighed.

"Did you get any cakes?" a voice asked in Lu-canian. Myro felt herself trembling; she had heard no footsteps. "Oh, I came down that wall," the speaker continued, delighted to have startled her; it was a small boy of about nine, an age that she particularly disliked, completely covered with dust. "Yes," she tried to answer indifferently, yet the face reminded her of someone. Then she recognized him; it was the urchin who had sat on the dolphin that morning and had winked at her as she had passed.

"Yes!" He imitated Myro's pronunciation. "But you're not from here, where do you come from?"

Myro spoke some Lucanian that a fisherman had taught her, but it was a softer dialect than the moun-tain tongue and mixed with foreign words. "From Sele," she said, as they had agreed to do if ques-tioned. "Why are you not at the Games?"

"I! At the Games! But I'm not a Lucanian." The

boy turned his head so that she could see the slave mark on his ear.

"Then why don't you talk Greek?"

"Greek? I don't know any. Where should I have learned it? In Poseidonia now we must speak Lucanian."

"From your mother," Myro suggested.

"Oh, she died of fever. My father was killed beside the Temple steps. With a spear. I passed the place again this morning. It is an ordinary, dusty stone like all the others."

Myro looked at the child more carefully; she was almost sorry for him. He was also, she decided, the dirtiest object that she had ever seen in her life. "What is your name?" she asked.

"Menis, son of Kleiton. I belong to one of the Commander's Guard," he added almost proudly.

He was thin, but not too thin. Myro judged that he increased his meals by stealing what food he wanted. "How many cakes did you get this morning?" she inquired.

"Only two." The tone was extremely mournful because Menis had learned that it paid to make people sorry for him, but he had actually snatched three and a fragment out of various baskets. "The slave in my master's kitchen knew my mother," he added. "She is kind to me, but there is never enough to eat." He stared at her so hopefully that Myro put her hand into the small goatskin bag swinging from her belt and brought out a piece of bread. It had no honey in it but it was better than the coarse Lucanian loaves, and Menis munched it gratefully. "Are you going to be a household slave?" she asked.

The child rubbed his ear. "My master won the swordsman's prize at the Games last year. He came back with a wound like that in his shoulder." Menis held his hands a palm's length apart. "I don't hate all the Lucanians. It is better to do things than to talk about them, but I was born free, so, naturally, when I am older, I shall run away."

"There are lots of wolves." As far as Myro knew, only a handful of fugitives had reached Salente during the eight years of exile, and of these, most were men from along the border.

"Yes, and they say the earth opens sometimes to swallow a traveller up or he is chased by men with claws instead of feet." Menis spoke slowly and distinctly so that the stranger should know how brave he was even to think of taking to the hills. "I don't like this brand on my ear," he grumbled, as if it were a new sort of ache.

"You had better grow a bit first." It had never occurred to Myro that she might be sorry for a boy; the Poseidonians irritated her, yet there was something about the child's desire to be free that made her feel the actual horror of this dead city instead of seeing it as the golden but hazy background of too-often repeated tales. "You could try to reach Sele," she suggested; "it is watched, but not so closely."

"If I got there, would you help me?"

"Of course, if I were still there; I am going to sea."

"I can count up to ten in Greek," Menis said, demonstrating on his fingers. He wanted to be friendly, and Myro laughed. Yet somehow she must get rid of him. If he saw Archias or heard the noise of the picks he might betray them innocently, and she wondered what to say. She tied the thongs of her bag but he took no notice. If she moved he would only follow her. "You're not listening," he said reprovingly, but at the moment Phila opened the door. "What are you doing here?" she shouted angrily at Menis, whom she evidently knew. "There is to be another distribution of cakes at the Temple."

"Only this evening, and the men are there now, talking of what they did before the war." Menis remembered a cuff he had got the previous summer from an irritated slave whom he had accidentally touched. He hung about hoping that the old woman would find him a morsel in the kitchen. "Run along," Phila ordered sharply a second time, "there isn't a crumb for either you or the dogs until I cook supper."

"See you at Sele!" Menis said cheerfully with a

wink at Myro as he trotted down the road. He turned down the next street, waited till he was sure that Phila was not following him, and then crept back into the deserted garden where the booming voice of Archias had wakened him from a sound sleep. Most of the house behind him was in ruins, but there was enough roof left in one corner for it to be used as a storeroom for jars of oil. There was grass growing between the stones and chips of marble strewn across the terrace. He climbed up the trunk of an old tree and lowered himself to the wall again, his heart beating with excitement. There were foreigners in Poseidonia! Somebody had said a stranger had called the battle cry. If that surly boy had come in from one of the villages, he would have been afraid to stray from his group, and would not have asked that foolish question about going to the Games. Could he be a messenger? There was a ship out in the bay. Was one of the Poseidonians trying to escape? A man was supposed to have got away the previous summer. The Lucanians had said that he had been drowned, but there was a rumor that some fishermen had hauled him out of the ocean with a boathook and that he had been helped on his way up the coast. He looked down cautiously. Phila was still there, shaking her head, and looking anxiously up and down the road as if she expected to see soldiers coming to fetch her at any moment. The boy below him muttered something, he took the old woman by the arm and led her into the house, then he came back himself and sat on the curb as if he too were on guard.

Phila returned to the courtyard, and as she saw Lykos leaning on his pick with his tunic sticking in damp patches to his back, seeming so old and yet so hopeful, she was ashamed of her selfishness. Why did she so ardently want to die within the city when he was so eager to live outside it? There was an empty hole in front of them and a quantity of loose soil on the ground.

"Let us try here," Lykos said gently, "this stone looks as if it had once been moved, it has sunk," and he tapped it. "It is not in line with the others."

"Nor is it two paces from the fountain."

Lykos shifted the point of his pick and inserted it under the longer stone. Unlike Phila, he had never doubted that Archias had buried the jar, but he knew the tricks that the most familiar objects could play on the senses. This block was smaller and easier to loosen. "I made a net once," he continued gently, hoping to soothe the gray-haired man beside him, "and I could have sworn by the gods that I had knotted every tenth mesh as usual. I must have been in love! The first time that the fisherman took it out he lost half of his catch. I had jumped the pattern and made three loops further apart at the fifteenth square. Of course, it sagged."

Archias was not listening. He began to pray

again. "I broke into the sanctuary. Even Cumae cannot cleanse me."

Lykos heaved desperately and got the stone out on its side. Was it imagination or was the soil less packed? He took the spade that Archias had dropped and struck something hard just under the surface. "Dig," he begged, because if the man went on making such a noise he would bring in the passers-by. "I've found either the treasure or a rock."

"It is more than two paces away."

"Not from the fountain," Lykos tried to conciliate his obstinate and confused companion, "you must measure it from the base and not the lions. Come, I need your help."

They put their tools down and scraped away the earth with their bare hands. A lump appeared that was the color of the soil but seemed to be the shape of a jar. Lykos took up his spade again and loosened the earth carefully; Archias lifted it up. "It is the jar," he said in a bewildered voice, "but it's not where I buried it. We are not two paces from the lions."

"You measured before from the animal's mouth," Lykos suggested; there was a look in the man's eyes that frightened him. "That is too far back, you must take it from the bottom of the fountain."

Archias set the clod of earth lovingly on the

bench. He was about to crack it apart when Lykos stopped him anxiously. "We must not open it here," he said, "it's late and we have to fill up the hole and sweep the pavement before anybody comes. Don't scatter dirt over the seat."

Phila went for a broom; they shovelled the earth away as rapidly as possible, and Lykos forgot the pain in his leg struggling with the larger of the stones. They tugged and swore until it fell into place again, after they had cracked a chip or two from the edges. Phila picked these up and tossed them into the fountain, but the second block was less easy. The stone sank, although they had tried to fill up the hole; they had to heave it up once more and fetch soil from under the rosebushes. Just as they were dropping it into position the second time they heard Myro shout. "Phila! Phila!" It was the signal that someone had returned.

"Hide!" Lykos pushed the triumphant man, who had both hands round the jar, into the hovel where they slept. "Be quiet," he added sternly, "do not move." He glanced hastily round; the stones were in place, but the soil was scattered everywhere. Had the steward returned by some trick of fate and caught them at the moment of apparent triumph? He limped to the doorway as quickly as his leg allowed to find Phila clutching the shoulders of Agathias, one of their fellow slaves.

"What is the matter with your wife? Is she ill?"

"A touch of the sun." Phila pretended to stagger.

"She fell into my arms," Agathias said, looking at them both suspiciously.

"It was the prayers, they were very long," Lykos explained. How could he get the man away? In his present state of irresponsible excitement Archias might come bounding out at any moment with the jar in his hands. "Go and lie down," he ordered Phila, in a harsher tone than he had ever used during their life together, "and let me have an hour in peace. What happened at the market place, Agathias, was there any news?"

"News! What news could there be for us slaves? They say some fool screamed the battle cry. Did you hear it?"

"I heard a shout but I did not know what it was."

"That procession ought to be stopped. The women start moaning and remembering; it does them no good and makes it worse for us afterwards. If you consider it carefully, what did we lose? I was a porter at the harbor, free to labor in summer and starve in winter. Now I get my food no matter what the weather is, and the steward isn't a bad master if a man is willing to work." He looked arrogantly at Lykos, expecting to be contradicted.

"It could be worse," Lykos agreed, in apparent gaiety. "They gave me two obols last night. Come and drink them up with me."

"Two obols?" Agathias smiled; the steward had

given him ten. They had handed the man a beggar's dole instead of the customary gift; it was another sign that Lykos was to be sold. Still, if the poor fool wanted to give him a drink, why not? "There is a stall round the corner opened just for today, and a wall where we can sit." He glanced at his fellow slave's leg. "What have you been doing to your knee?"

Lykos glanced down; it was caked with earth. "Oh, these women! Phila made a poultice for it." He brushed the dirt away impatiently. "A drink will do me more good. Shall we go?" He stepped into the street.

"You had better take your stick."

"Oh, we can't get drunk on an obol apiece of wine." Lykos forced himself to laugh. "Phila," he shouted, "bring me my spear." It was a joke in the household that he leaned on his staff as if it were a weapon. "Hurry, where is the woman? They are never there if you want them." Phila bustled forward, like a bird flying out of a cavern bewildered by the light as he thought afterwards, and thrust the stick into his hand. Agathias turned down the street, whistling as he went. Lykos lingered a moment before he followed him. "Sweep the pavement and go to the priestess," he whispered. "I will join you as soon as I can."

Harmonia had fallen asleep. She was lying on the couch, an arm flung across her forehead, when

Archias, followed by Myro and Phila, burst noisily into the room.

"I found it! I found it!" He set the jar triumphantly on the nearest flat surface that he could find, the stool standing at his sister's elbow, as proud as a small boy who had come home with the season's first bunch of grapes.

"My lady, we were almost discovered." Phila was still trembling from the shock. "Agathias came before we had filled up the pavement and Lykos had to hold him at the door . . ." She choked, and Myro finished the sentence for her, "and take him to a wineshop while we escaped."

Archias did not need to crack the cover; the cords had rotted. He lifted it up, put his hand inside the jar, and pulled out a bulky package wrapped up in moldy linen. "Our necklace!" The excited words burst from Harmonia's mouth, and for the flash of a second she remembered how hard the gold circlet round her mother's neck had seemed to a child's hands and how the carved beads had clung to the white robe as gracefully as butterflies. Her brother put two brooches, a chain, and a bag stuffed full of coins on top of it, then he took out a silver object, tarnished but unscratched. He rubbed away a speck of earth from the shoulders of Poseidon and held it up in triumph. "Safe," he roared. "Now we can found our city, now we can cross the sea."

It would not be Poseidonia, Phila thought. Men might call it by that name but it would be different, an echo, the memory some girl kept of her home after she had followed her husband to another land. It would be better to let it die rather than to transplant it, it was old as she was now, and neither prayer nor plant could give youth back to them. Archias turned the disk round in his fingers; it was no bigger than the palm of his hand, but the god's hair was blowing in the wind, in that soft breeze that would fill the sails that evening whether they reached the ship of Krantas or not. Even the dolphin leaping out of the silver ocean was not afraid of the trident, it was free.

Archias looked round impatiently. Why had the jar been found under the wrong stone? Was it a sign that the gods were still angry with him? He wondered for the first time since he had begun the journey if death were waiting for him here in these doomed streets while he dusted the jewels and dropped them into the pilgrim's bag that he still wore strapped to his belt. His hands moved awkwardly; he let a coin slip, and Myro picked it up for him. The walls seemed to be closing in as if he were back in that cave, his breath came in gasps. "Get your cloak," he said sharply to his sister, "we have not a moment to lose."

"And my husband?" Phila protested indignantly. Lykos had found the treasure, had prevented Agathias from surprising them, and now this crazy fool was ready to abandon him to his fate. "I will try to

100

find him," Myro assured her hastily because she had seen a wild look come into the Greek's eyes, but at that moment there was a knock at the door. "We are trapped," Archias yelled, feeling for the knife that dangled under his tunic, but whoever it was tapped lightly again, and then Lykos came into the room. "It took me a long time to get rid of the man," he grumbled, "and all the coins I had. I heard the flutes as I came down the road. Are you ready, my lady? We must start."

"As soon as they pass . . . they do pass here?" Archias questioned.

Harmonia nodded. "We must follow the procession till we can mingle with the fishermen."

"They will know that we are strangers."

"But they will not betray a fellow Poseidonian."

Everybody but Archias laughed. "For a slice of bread, for half a rotten olive," Lykos quoted grimly the local proverb.

"The fugitive who reached us at Salente said that that was how he escaped last year."

"He was one and we are five." Lykos balanced his stick as if it were a spear. "Still, no other way is open to us."

Harmonia picked up the mirror from the ledge beside her. Like the necklace, it had belonged to her mother, but it was an everyday possession, and the limbs of the nymph that formed the handle were dented and rubbed. It was all that was left to her of her home; she could not leave it behind, and she slipped it with a couple of trifles into the bag that she had already fastened to her waist. Archias was busy stuffing bread on the top of the disk, in case, she supposed, some guard wanted to know what he was carrying. "I have found your veil," Phila said; she helped the priestess to arrange it over her hair, and Myro brought her a tattered winter cloak. The flutes were drawing nearer, Lykos beckoned impatiently, and she glanced hastily round at the walls of what had virtually been her cell. How much she had suffered here! Yet the compassion of Hera had filled the room that morning with its peace. New experiences were waiting for her, and other sorrows; for the moment her mind was numb and she walked through the doorway after her brother without turning her head.

The sun would set in another hour, their masters would return, the holiday would be over. "Let them pass," Archias said anxiously as the flute players went by; "we are lost if they recognize you." Harmonia nodded; her face was now completely hidden by the veil. She tried to stoop, and this was easy because, between the weight of the statue and her great cloak, she felt almost too faint to stand, yet she had officiated at so many ceremonies that it seemed impossible to become part of this crowd without some women noticing her and calling by name.

It was a short procession. The stragglers were too weary to sing. They shuffled on, their bare backs marked by the whip, apathetic, dirty, and neglected. It was not worship, it was the distribution of the few cakes left over from the morning service that drew them to the Temple. "Look," Phila whispered. An unkempt woman who had been Harmonia's playfellow slipped past. She had grown up in a palace with a servant of her own; now her face was as wrinkled as a wolf's muzzle, and no patch could hold the rents in her chiton together. Was that child behind her Kleiton's son? Harmonia recognized the snub nose and the thick, manelike hair. Poor Kleiton, on the day that she had entered the Temple he had vowed never to marry, only to wed a friend of hers before the year was out! He had died with a spear through his heart during the last rush near the steps. Now his boy, the urchin could not be more than nine, was dirtier than a beggar and branded on the ear.

She did not notice Menis wink at Phila, nor did she see him wriggle out of the ranks further down the street. Was Salente a trap, would Nikias have called her vision of that morning as imaginary as her brother's fears? She looked along the lines; the women were old, there was hardly a young head among them, only some children eager for the

cakes. "Come," she said with such authority that
Archias followed her meekly, although he had
planned to wait until the last straggler had passed.

> *"May the fields be gold,*
> *may the summer be merciful."*

The tired voices pleaded for a harvest that would
only benefit their conquerors. "We shall return in
triumph," Myro whispered confidently, "the city
is in your heart. It is not a strip of ground." Brave
words, but Myro spoke them because she had grown
up in freedom; would Kleiton's son have known
what they meant? The wall towered above them, no
longer a symbol of their greatness but a reminder
of their servitude. She walked slowly forward
among the women until they came to the turning
by the Gate, too exhausted now to notice anything
but the pebbles underfoot from the cracked pave-
ments and the fallen, slippery flowers.

The flute players turned toward the market place.
Harmonia could just see Demo's basket bobbing up
and down with the movement of her head. A stiff
figure, it must be Phanion, was standing on the
drum of a broken pillar, to watch them pass. Had
something happened? Demo broke away from the
attendants and to Harmonia's amazement ran toward the priest; then the crowd swayed together
in a confusion of waving arms and rags.

A small, dirty child sprang down from a wall

and raced up to the fugitives. "Run," Menis shouted, "I saw the woman recognize you. She is looking for the priest. Go."

Run! Run where? Harmonia felt the lash of Phanion's triumph. He would destroy the figure, Archias would die. She would not even have that gift because he would keep her alive to watch her misery, and she had forgotten the hemlock, which was steeping in a pot beside her bed. Whatever happened, she would never see that quiet room again. She looked round wildly and caught sight of Fabricius, who was on guard beside the wall.

Hera, and Hera only, inspired her next movement. She flung back her cloak, lifted up the statue, and advanced toward the middle of the gateway, chanting the morning hymn in a low voice, to the consternation of her companions.

Fabricius stepped forward. The group had no authority to go outside the walls as far as he knew, but he was a superstitious man and had no wish to anger the gods, even if they were not his own, by disturbing a religious ceremony. He lifted his hand but not his spear.

"We take the Lady to her dwelling," Harmonia chanted, staring at the outstretched palm as if in utter surprise. "Let us pass. We are due at the Temple by sunset."

Fabricius looked from one member of the party to the other. The priestess had dignity and power, but the tattered attendants and the wild-eyed man were like scarecrows, and he wondered again how Philinna's mother could have let the girl mingle with such a horde of slaves. "Have you permission?" he asked.

Harmonia held out the token that she had already shown that morning; but, as she hoped, it did not occur to him that she had kept it during the day. Fabricius hesitated. He turned the metal over in his hand; it was strange that nobody had given him fresh orders, but he did not want to disturb the captain who was playing dice in the guardroom, and only a Lucanian official could have issued it.

"Go then, but speedily. We shut the Gate in an hour."

Harmonia bowed gravely. She continued to hold the statue up as they walked through the archway, then softly, because she knew as well as Fabricius that his captain was sitting less than twenty paces away, she began the triumphant song that always marked the end of the spring festival. Her exhaustion had vanished, she felt like a young girl.

"We are saved!" Lykos whispered, but he dared not take his wife's arm, lest the sentinel should be watching them.

Archias looked back at the wall. Rosemary was growing out of the dents that had been made by Lucanian arrows. The stones reminded him of a gray wave, apparently smooth but actually full of linklike ripples and knots. "The Gate to the Sea," he shouted, pointing at the archway, "it was always the way to freedom." This time there were no flames, and his sister was by his side.

"Be quiet," Harmonia interrupted, "we are still in great danger. Tell me, child, what did you actually see?"

"I knew they were strangers." Menis pointed at her brother and his attendant. "I wanted to escape as well so I followed them all the way from the Commander's house until I lost you in the crowd. When I saw the boy at the corner"—he jerked his head toward Myro—"I climbed up a wall to see passed, and I saw her recognize you. I don't like what you would do. The woman with the basket her. She slapped my face the other morning because I caught her talking to old Phanion under an archway, and I watched her run up to him when they got to the steps. We have a little time," he spoke with great assurance, "they will search the Temple first."

"Follow me, there used to be a short cut here." Archias left the path and strode off across the sands; they had been familiar to him in boyhood. A dozen gulls flew over his right shoulder toward the bay; as he watched them the voices that had been ringing in his ears died into a quiet murmur. "For-given . . ." The Oracle had answered him, "for-given. . . ." He remembered racing downhill between the lightning flashes, but now the memory was blurred, the terror had vanished. He need go to sea no more, he could take the gold that had belonged to his father and return to Cumae, to the priests. Perhaps the physician who had interpreted his oracle would tell him why the treasure had been six, and not two, paces from the lions? They might even let him take Myro with him; she was a strange child, but she understood his moods. Harmonia would have her mother's jewels, she would be rich; Iphion and his wife would welcome her to their home. Everything was turning out as he had prophesied, and those fools at Salente had called him mad! He almost ran forward; his eyes were on the ship; the bag had become so heavy that he was holding it under his arm. "Hurry!" he yelled, then, hearing no answer, he turned round. The others had been unable to keep up with his long strides and were stumbling along some distance behind.

"Hurry!" he shouted again. "They may send chariots after us."

"No, they are all at the Games," Lykos answered. He was hopping and struggling forward with the help of his stick, but the lameness had increased, and Phila was panting and tired.

"There is no time," Archias said almost angrily as they came nearer to him. "Come with me, Harmonia, it will be easier to walk once we reach the edge of the sea." The walls were golden in the setting sun, the shore was still empty. There was nothing on the salt-encrusted dunes but their own shadows.

"Take Myro and go to the boat," Harmonia suggested, "it has to be found and refloated."

"I will not leave you," Myro answered firmly. In Salente she had imagined the priestess to be like one of her devout old aunts, who would not eat this, that, or the other food lest it be displeasing to the gods. Now she had seen her, she knew that Harmonia was the true greatness of which the exiles dreamed; she had all her brother's fire and none of his petulance.

"Yes, Myro, it is the way that you can help me most."

Myro shook her head. Once they separated they might never see each other again; besides, who knew what Archias might begin, he was capable of turning around and going back to Poseidonia to remeasure the space between the lions in that courtyard. She looked up at Harmonia's face, which was calm, the lips drawn slowly upwards as if there were no wisdom that they had not tasted, and replied, "I am staying with you whatever you say."

"You must leave us, lady," the netmaker said quietly. "Perhaps we can use that instead of the hemlock," he added, as a sluggish viper crawled away among the stones.

"In my day there were not all these snakes,"

Archias complained, as if he had not noticed that the huts had been burnt down and the wrestling-grounds destroyed.

"Phanion will believe Demo"—Lykos spat on the palm of his blistered hand—"but they will have to have evidence to convince the Guard. Not all the people will help them, and even if they find your room is empty, they will suppose you are hidden in the Temple and many will object if the sanctuary is searched."

"We have no time," Archias repeated obstinately. "Here, take my stick as well, Lykos, you will walk more quickly with it." They followed Archias in amazement, wondering how he could remember the twists and turns of this almost obliterated path after so many years. It was still a mile to the shrine, and Harmonia kept turning her head; she saw themselves surrounded by soldiers, mocking and shouting, long before they could reach the boat. Then deep under her fears, like her brother, she remembered the Oracle. "Come"—she took Phila by the arm—"a little haste now and we can rest for a lifetime afterwards."

"Is it much further?" Menis panted. His legs were short, he had been running about all day, and he was very, very hungry. Nobody answered; they were stretched out now in an uneven line, Archias in front, the women in the middle, and the lame Greek swinging almost swiftly along with the help of the two sticks. The sand got into their sandals or slithered away in long, paddle-shaped furrows; they were not walking in the direction that Harmonia had taken that morning but directly toward the sea. Myro had taken Phila's other arm; she was not thinking but only counting steps, ten to the withered bush, twenty more to the cracked piece of rock, as far as from her father's house to the wharf, to bring them to the beach.

"I see them," Menis screamed. "Look at the dust at the Gate!"

"You must leave us," Lykos said, taking Phila's hand. "Run, you still have a chance."

"It is too late," Harmonia said breathlessly. "You were right, Phila, I wish I had the hemlock."

The Guard, running in formation, was pouring out of the city. They could see the sentinels pointing to them from the top of the wall. Even a bird could not have hidden itself on these bleak dunes; they could not hope to reach the boat. "To the sea," Archias shouted, "it is better to drown than to be captured."

She had never felt more alive, Myro thought, as they raced toward the bay. The air was fresh after the midday heat; a tiny yellow flower pushed its way out of the sand. Why had Archias insisted upon digging up that disk? It was his sister, it was people who mattered, not their symbols. They should have rushed her away from the shrine before the procession had arrived. Of course she was proud of having been inside Poseidonia, but Myro knew with a clarity born of extreme danger that no success would alter the family verdict. If she reached the ship what future would be for her at Salente other than to accompany Archias on his journeys? It was better to die; but no, she wanted Harmonia to be safe. Her breathing choked her, not from running but through anger; the exiles had lost their city because they had resisted changes with the stubbornness that they should have shown toward their enemies. "To the sea," Archias kept yelling. Myro could not fling her thoughts far enough forward to imagine nonexistence; she could merely remember the savage force of the huge wave that had almost overturned them, was it only that morning?

There was a hoarse yell. "They are gaining on us," Archias cried. The first runners were not more than a few hundred paces away.

Only a small sandhill separated them from the sea. Still in front, Archias rushed to the top of the slope, and stopped. "Trapped!" Lykos muttered; they must have sent soldiers from another district. The struggle with Agathias flashed into his mind, and he thought sorrowfully of how near they had been to safety. Then, as he drew level with Archias, he saw a boat drawn up on the sand with a sailor beside it and another figure coming toward them.

"Krantas!" Myro and Harmonia shouted together.

"I believed Archias. I knew he would fetch you." The beard was gray but the round face and smiling eyes had not changed since Harmonia had last seen him. "We have been rowing up and down for an hour in case you needed help. We saw you running across the dunes."

"They are following us."

"Yes, and from both sides." Three chariots were racing toward them, although they were still some distance away. The black and scarlet harness of the horses matched the stiff feathers of the drivers' helmets; they could hear the thud of the wheels. It was sunset. The Lucanians were returning from the Games.

Even Phila found the last few paces easy. The ground was firm, the sailor had his shoulder to the boat. There was not time for Harmonia to remember that she was leaving Poseidonia forever; she scrambled aboard and helped the old woman follow her. Somebody dragged Lykos over the stern; Archias picked Menis up and dropped him beside Harmonia, wet to the waist, as if he were a puppy. The bottom stuck for a moment, then she felt the craft floating under her as the rowers pulled violently through the surf. She was not afraid, there was something friendly about the rush of water. Poseidon would be kind to them. Was the city not under his protection? She clung to the edge of her seat as they soared up and forward until, just as they reached the crest, her brother stopped rowing and shouted, "My boat, it is there by the rushes, I have to go back for it."

"Pull," Krantas yelled, "you'll upset us, pull!" It was as if they were on top of a waterfall; the planks shivered, they rode down into a hollow, rolled again, and rose upon a shieldlike surface of blue sea with the ship less than a quarter of an hour away in front of them.

"My boat," Archias wailed.

"It will be useless to the Lucanians if they find it. It was very old."

"I don't want them touching anything I own."

"Oh, Krantas," Harmonia interrupted, "you seem to spend your days rescuing us, we could never have got to the rushes in time."

"I was glad to set foot on my native sand but equally glad to leave it again." Krantas pointed to the group of soldiers and chariots that was gathering by the shore.

"Have they got javelins?" Lykos asked with a note of fear in his voice.

More chariots had arrived. The foot soldiers and the drivers were mixed up together; some were on their knees examining the footprints in the sand, one or two were crawling into the dunes with their shields held above their heads. "They think an army has landed," Krantas added with amusement. "They will stand watch all night."

"Somebody is pointing at us!" Phila screamed.

"Let them, they have no boat."

"Even if they find that old barrel Archias hid in the rushes, they cannot catch up with us. It is too slow."

"It was not a barrel," Archias protested indignantly, "it was a solidly built craft."

"I think I see Lucullus." Lykos gave a quick backward glance. "I should know the three scarlet feathers on the helmet anywhere, they have nodded at me so often." It was the Commander. He stood giving orders with his hand on the rim of a chariot, and a messenger started to run back toward the town.

"There is no need to be frightened now, Phila." It seemed to Harmonia that her words came from far away, a different person in another time. "We shall be aboard our ship in a few moments."

"Yes, you are free again," Lykos said, swinging to and fro with the pull of the oars, and his wife nodded. She did not want to spoil his happiness, but she knew that she would always be afraid, just as the starfish that was ripped from its rock scented and dreaded the next storm. She stared back at the mountains, trying to fix every outline in her mind, the dip, the serpentine furrow, the twin peaks that rose like lily stems that had for some reason never flowered, the lower slopes that were a tawny, animal gold. "They will cure you at Salente," she muttered, remembering how she had nursed Lykos and lied to him because after the Sack there had been no physicians for slaves. "Is there not said to be a stream in the north, my lady," she appealed to Harmonia, "where all who bathe are healed?"

"I shall never bring you another olive crown," Lykos interrupted sorrowfully—the muscles were withered, and though they might ease the stiffness, nothing could cure the limb—"but I will tell you one thing, Phila, never believe the philosophers who say that we learn through suffering. I have never accepted either my lameness or our slavery. I have endured but resented them, every waking hour."

Otherwise the pair would not have survived, Harmonia thought, but nothing was rigid, every individual had to find his particular law. If she had to face the Sack and make her decision over again, she would still choose to stay. Whatever had been the cause of the disaster, it had been right at that time to share the fortunes of her fellow citizens. "Things change," she murmured but so softly that nobody else heard her, and for a wild moment she wished that instead of going to Salente she could float forever across these calm, indifferent waves.

There was a hail; this time it was a friendly voice. A rope was flung to them, smiling faces looked down from the ship, everybody talked at once. "Lykos!" A sailor stretched his arms joyfully over the rail as if he could have bridged the depth below to haul his former comrade aboard.

"I found it!" Archias held the disk up in the air, but the crew was more interested in the survivors and news of their friends, and he turned with a worried air toward his sister. "I must go back to the priest. I must know why it was almost six paces from the lions."

"All things have an end," Harmonia said wearily, putting her hand upon her brother's arm. "Isn't it enough to have brought the symbol back? Remember, at Cumae they told you to be happy."

There was a moment of confusion, then they began to climb a rope ladder up to the deck. If only Kleiton could know that his son was free, the priestess thought, watching the child's feet going up the rungs in front of her; but even if something of the spirit survived, as Nikias had believed, it would be far away; the boy was alone. He was so young that they might be able to do something about his ear. "Hold tight!" Myro commanded, and Harmonia realized that she had been standing on the same step for several moments. Was there a ship? Was this only a dream? Then Krantas, who had run up first, reached down his hand and she felt herself standing beside him on planks that swayed gently as the vessel moved. "Is everyone aboard?" The children were beside her, Phila was sitting on the deck, Lykos and the sailor drew themselves over the rail, and her brother was showing the disk to anyone whose cloak he could catch. She heard them hoisting the anchor, they were bending the sails, and now the last green ribbon disappeared from the sky.

"Come and eat, Harmonia," Archias called gaily. She noticed Menis sitting cross-legged by her brother with half a loaf of bread in one hand and a large piece of cheese in the other, and that must be Myro's voice, asserting gravely, "Oh, apart from the Temple it was a dusty, disappointing place." Then she walked to the stern, although it was too black to distinguish one building from another, to look in vain for some familiar roof. Someday she might understand the purpose of their suffering, sitting perhaps in a garden at Salente with—and how strange it would be—nothing to fear. At the moment she clung a little unsteadily to a rope, the wind was rising, and she could hear Archias laughing in the boisterous way in which he had roared as a boy. The past was over; some intuition told her that a recognition of this fact was the purpose of her liberation; she had to persuade the exiles that it was false to dream of a return and that they must root themselves in the new region that had offered them shelter with such willingness. She stared across the bay: there was their beach outlined by a rim of foam. Was that the sound of a trumpet calling up more troops? Then as a welcome darkness blotted out the city, she saw in the last flash of light the towers and the white gateway through which they had passed to freedom, old, indestructible, facing the masterless sea.